THREE NIGHTS BEFORE CHRISTMAS

A Love Story for Pet Lovers

Daphne Lynn Stewart

Copyright © 2024 Daphne Lynn Stewart

All rights reserved

The characters and events portrayed in this book are fictitious. Any similarity to real persons, living or dead, is coincidental and not intended by the author.

No part of this book may be reproduced, or stored in a retrieval system, or transmitted in any form or by any means, electronic, mechanical, photocopying, recording, or otherwise, without express written permission of the publisher.

ISBN-13: 9798345742662

Cover design by: Deborah Cannon

Printed in the United States of America

For Beatrice
In loving memory of Lily

CHAPTER 1

Some people bring out the best in you; some people bring out the worst. Charlie brought out the best in me so why had this happened?

A blue sliver of light shot across the bed. In a few minutes it would be daybreak. I stabbed the darkness with blurry eyes searching for consciousness. I was sweating and my heart threatened to leap out of my chest. I had dreamed that the diamond in my engagement ring had cracked in half.

Was my perfect life only a dream? No. It was real. Charlie was still here sound asleep with his dog Lily, on the other side of his head. I could hear the reassuring rhythm of his breathing and Lily gently snoring beside him.

He called her his little lump of love. I must concede she is adorable—a sweet, furry, doe-eyed lump of affection. So, what did that make me? His *big* lump of love? Not that I was particularly big. I would say I was average size. But I am probably not awake enough to think clearly. The point is—he had hesitated when I asked, "If Lily is your little lump of love, what does that make me?" Naturally, I was joking. But that split second of dead quiet disturbed me. People had a surprisingly strong attachment to their dogs.

We had known each other only a short while, but when he got down on bended knee and asked me to twine my future to his, I knew if I married him, I would also be marrying his dog.

I had said yes without hesitation.

His snowflake nightlight was creating faint swirling patterns against the walls in the darkness. He was a sucker for Christmas, and me? I just couldn't quite get into it. Our family was not big on the festive season. Ever since I could remember, we had always spent the holidays in Florida.

Charlie was up now and gone to work. Lily sat on the floor whining for 'second breakfast'. I rolled out of bed in my ice blue silk pajamas, daylight streaming through the gaps in the drawn curtains and stared at my ring.

My job was in Toronto and although my hometown of Dundas was only an hour away, I long ago decided that I hated the commute, so I had moved to make things convenient. You never knew when a traffic jam or a multi-car pileup was going to make you late for work. Sweet considerate man that he was, Charlie agreed.

I had a gorgeous luxury condo in Toronto, but I had returned to my hometown for the holidays. My boss had challenged the idea of my taking time off from my designs. But finally, he had admitted that I deserved a week's vacation. He warned me however that my big spring project was dependent upon my winning approval for one particular job. The customer was a difficult one, very fussy and argumentative. If I wanted to win the bid, I would have to create something that would blow her away. So, I had brought my laptop with me. And my work.

I refused to disappoint my parents however. This year Mom and Dad had skipped Florida in order to spend Christmas with me. I mean—this was a first! Christmas at home, oh my. And they wanted to have Charlie over. So that was the reason I was here in Dundas. That was where my parents lived—in a mansion overlooking the conservation lands. Dundas was also where my fiancé lived—but minus the mansion. Charlie owned a small, quaint Victorian style house with a lovely, treed backyard within walking distance of the main shopping street.

The ring was intact. The diamond had not cracked. I turned my back on the window and wrapped my matching robe around myself and headed for the vanity mirror in the adjoining bathroom. The sight of my face in the smudged mirror brought it all back. Thank goodness there was no one to see me cringe at the memory.

Ugh. My eyes still smarted from the stupid thing I had done after dinner last evening. How I could have been so stupid I don't know, but now humiliation was getting the best of me.

"It's okay, Sophie," Charlie had reassured me. "You are overreacting. You didn't do it on purpose."

I found it difficult to believe him. I should believe him. But how could it be okay? Here I was, VP of the landscape design division of a multinational architectural corporation, and I had pepper sprayed myself—and my fiancé's dog.

My eyes burned when I blinked, but that was the least of my concerns. I was worried about Lily. She had stopped wheezing after the incident but the effects were still visible. Her eyes like mine were red.

Charlie had left a message with his vet last night and there was a text on my phone from him right now.

> ***Appointment at 10:00 am.***
> ***Please be prompt.***
> ***And don't worry. I'm not mad at you.***

I had promised to take her. Holy Moses. I slapped down the lid of my laptop where I was about to go over the plans I had drawn up last week. It was nine already. The phone suddenly chimed. The Call Display said that it was my mother.

"Hi Mom," I said. "Can't talk now. I'm late for an

appointment."

"Fine, dear, but don't forget our shopping trip this afternoon. Where shall we meet?"

"The Carnegie Gallery?" I suggested.

"Good choice. See you then."

I had better get a move on. I jumped in the shower, tried to avoid getting my hair wet and leaped out after a minor rinse. As usual the red plastic shower curtain was on the wrong side of the tub and I managed to get the tiny brown and beige bathroom (oh, how I detested those colors!) thoroughly wet.

I hoped Charlie realized that when we were married—if he still wanted to marry me after that disaster last night—we would have to have a much larger bathroom. And a glassed-in shower stall. Plus, the entire thing would have to be designed in colors more pleasing to the eye.

My toes landed in a puddle of water. No time to mop. I tossed the used red towels onto the floor (for the record, they *did* match the ugly shower curtain), scuffled around with my bare feet then went for my state-of-the-art Dyson Airwrap styler. It dried any unintended damp hair in seconds and curled the rest in less than three minutes. Sure, it wasn't salon perfect, but it would have to do. The dog came first and she was scratching on the door wondering what was taking Mama so long, and yes, where was second breakfast?

I left the steamy bathroom and crooned at Lily,

who was wagging her feathery tail. "Come on baby. Mummy has to get dressed. You can have second breakfast in the car."

I buttoned a white cotton blouse to collarbone level and tugged on a black, gray and white, soft wool cardigan, overtop my black designer jeans. Then it was gray leather ankle boots to which I had to sit down on the bottom step and tug them on before zippering them up, and a powder pink wool wrap coat with an oversized cashmere scarf in pearl gray that I snatched off the foyer hall hook after I rose and ran for the door. Charlie always said I dressed for appearances and not for practical purposes. He was correct in every way. But I had no other kinds of clothes. He was the fur papa. I was just the weekend fur mama.

As head landscape architect, I worked for the corporation *Inside Outside*, and had to dress the part.

We had wealthy clients. And when I say wealthy, I mean *really* rich clients. You know the people who inhabited the multimillion-dollar estates along the lakeside? Those were our clients. Their landscaping were modern, state-of-the-art outside spaces designed to bring the indoors outdoors by emulating elements of their surroundings i.e. forest and lake. They were the most beautiful *un*natural natural spaces you could imagine. Yup. That was my job.

Charlie on the other hand owned a mid-sized

local gardening center. He normally catered to individuals, not corporations. But one time when I failed to locate the exact botanical features I was seeking Charlie swaggered up to me while I was visiting his garden center and charmed me with a selection of alternative plantings. These varieties were like nothing I would have thought of on my own. His quick thinking and innovative ideas helped me transform a staid old rose garden into a modern outdoor experience of terraced, stone walkways leading down to a sunken garden of fairylike wildflowers.

That was how we met.

It was love at first sight. And an engagement on second sight.

Now in hindsight, I am wondering if we moved too fast.

It's not that I don't love him. Because I do. But we barely knew each other. He was a dog person and I had never owned a dog. In fact, my mom was allergic, so that was why. My dad would have bought me a dog in an instant otherwise. Instead, he bought me a car. When I was sixteen that is.

But none of this matters. I had to get Charlie's dog to the vet, pronto.

In the car, I belted her in. Charlie insisted on that. I passed a handful of doggy cookies from a half-opened bag to her eager mouth. With Lily occupied with second breakfast, I returned to the hood of my satin gray Lexus and began scraping off the snow.

The windshield was frosted and the wiper blades stuck to the glass. This was what happened when you parked outside for lack of a garage. In Toronto I had underground parking.

I chipped away until I had scraped two squares through which I could see. That I could *even* see—the state my eyes were in—was a miracle in itself. Those two peepholes, one on the driver's side and the other on the passenger side, would have to do. Hopefully the rest of last night's weather would melt on the way. I was late already.

I popped on my designer sunglasses, took them off again to polish them, returned them to my face and backed out of the snowy driveway onto the bright slushy road in my SUV. The salt trucks had done their job early this morning.

If I kept the shades on no one would notice, but would they ask why I was wearing sunglasses on a cloudy day?

The Spencer Creek Animal Hospital was only three minutes away. Ordinarily I would have walked, but I was late. Traffic was light. And despite the absence of sun last night's snow was glaringly bright. I pulled into the parking lot and found a space right outside the front doors. As I yanked the glass door wide to allow Lily to precede me, her long feathers mopping the ground, my corner vision caught the spray-painted images of dogs and cats decked out in Christmas gear on the windows.

No Santa hat for dear Lily; she would never tolerate it. Yes, I have tried. Believe me I have tried. Some pets truly believe that dog clothes are a form of animal cruelty.

At reception I was informed that Lily's usual vet was off for the holidays but someone else would sub for her. I was nervous and for good reason, probably more so than Lily. She curled up underneath a chair while I paced towards a bulletin board on the wall. There were the usual grooming-services posters, and missing-pet and dogs-needing-adoption notices. One of the flyers caught my eye, a Cavalier requiring a home.

Hi! My name is Rosie. I'm seven years old.
I have a sweet personality.
I am very trusting and friendly.
Please take me home.

I was oddly taken by this dog. A troubling flip had occurred in the vicinity of my chest. Was this again a consequence of the pepper gas? Consuming peppers could cause me to suffer esophageal spasms. Which was why I never ate them.

We were called into the examining room, a well-scoured, disinfectant smell greeting us as we approached one of two chairs to wait. Lily was nervous. Like most dogs, a visit to the vet was not much fun. Someone was going to poke you and prod you in places they had no business being, and then they would stick you with a needle or give you something bad-tasting to eat.

"It's all right darling," I whispered, crouching to lift her onto my lap. I stopped myself just in time when I realized my coat was light-colored. I had no time to take my coat to the dry cleaner. "The nice lady just wants to make sure there is no permanent damage from last night's fiasco."

Her response to my reassurances was to shake moisture from dragging her feathers along the wet sidewalk all over my boots. I guess it's time to explain what I mean about feathers. Of course, dogs don't have feathers the way birds do. But Cavaliers have long feathery hair that grows along their sides, chests, legs and tails and some even to their feet. These are what breeders refer to as feathers.

The shaking reminded me how wet she was underneath. Best to leave her on the floor. I went over to the counter by the sink where a box of tissues stood and removed two or three. I wiped down Lily's tummy. Then I snatched a few more, and rubbed my hands clean, tossed the soiled tissues into a convenient trashcan and sat down holding Lily's leash while she settled half under the chair at my boots.

When the doctor walked in my breath caught. I knew Lily's regular vet was off for the Christmas holidays, but I wasn't expecting to recognize her substitute. Why my heart rate increased I don't exactly know. It was the same reaction as when I had glimpsed the picture of the black and tan

Cavalier in the waiting area. Maybe it was because I knew it seemed weird that I hadn't removed my sunglasses. But if you saw how I looked minus them you would understand why.

The vet wasn't a woman, it was a man, and surprisingly, he recognized me behind the shades.

CHAPTER 2

"Sophie? Sophie Star, is that you?"

No point in denying it. If he recognized me with my sunglasses on, he would certainly recognize me without them. I masked my embarrassment with a broad smile. "Leo? Leo MacVee? *You're* the vet?"

"Just for the holidays. I'm renovating my clinic. Had to clear out for a couple of weeks. So, I was able to sub for the Spencer Creek hospital. In the new year I'll be back in business." His eyes gave me the once over. "Wow. Long time no see. Back in town to visit your parents? How are they? How are you?"

"I am—I'm good." I glanced down at Lily by my feet. "As long as *she* is."

I managed to collect myself and not fall over from unexpectedly seeing my high school sweetheart in his white veterinarian lab coat. Leo and I had dated in the latter part of high school. We broke up when I went to do my masters degree in landscape architecture at the University of British Columbia in Vancouver, and he went to the Ontario Veterinary College in Guelph. It was an amicable breakup. In fact, to this day, I'm not sure who broke up with whom or if it was mutual. At one time, throughout those six years we were together, I honestly thought he was *the* one. He always believed we would get married one day. In fact, he'd been planning our life together since we were in high school. I recall, one time, as we were driving through a ritzy neighborhood, the huge houses shadowed by heavy, mature trees, he asked if I wanted to start planning a house. I had stared at him in disbelief. And as the shadows lengthened and deepened, my thoughts darkened. I hadn't even started university yet, hadn't decided what I wanted to do with my life. It was at that moment I believe I realized that he had probably already picked out names for our future children, and decided on how many we would have.

It was only seconds later that I also realized I had never thought about having children. At least, not with him. But then, why on earth would those thoughts enter my mind; I was eighteen.

Despite that, as I looked at him with fresh eyes, I could definitely see what I had seen in him back then.

He was always single-minded and organized. While most teenagers had dreams with no clue as how to achieve them, Leo had single-minded goals.

These goals—like finishing high school, doing a bachelor's degree in science and then competing for scholarships to attend Veterinary College—allowed him to turn his goals into a dream. His dream was to become an animal doctor and he had accomplished that. I had no doubt that he applied this strategy to everyday life. Everything he ever wanted he had probably obtained. In that we were compatible.

"How are you?" he asked, abruptly intruding on my thoughts.

"Oh—ah—good," I replied.

There was an awkward silence because our reunion was such a surprise. For the life of me I had not thought about him in years.

"So… do you live in Dundas now?" I stammered.

"Ancaster," he answered.

So that particular plan had come to fruition. He had always meant to have a house in Ancaster, the town adjacent to Dundas. Were his kids named Marilyn, Samantha and David? I wondered. Probably not the most appropriate time to ask.

He watched me fuss with my scarf, as I remained tongue-tied, mistaking my speechlessness for indifference. I was not indifferent. God no, I was not. In fact, I was desperately curious. And wondering why, just as I was having doubts about my own relationship, he had shown up in my life.

He took my silence as a cue to get down to

business. His gaze skimmed the chart he held in his left hand before setting it on the counter. He bent over to greet Lily. "Let's see what we have here. You have a really pretty pup in this little Cavalier."

"Thanks," I said. "But she's not mine. She's my fiancé's."

Why I felt the need to clarify troubled me. Of course, she was mine. At least she would be once Charlie and I were married.

Leo seemed unaware of my disquiet. He squatted and stretched out a hand. Lily approached bravely.

He lifted her onto the examining table and I rested my stomach against the edge to prevent her from trying to leap down. He was very practiced with dogs and she stopped fussing and allowed him to examine her.

I glanced down at the hand that was now petting her silky coat.

"The problem is with her eyes," I said, still staring at his hand. He had a platinum wedding band on his third left-hand finger. So, he *was* married. And were there children?

Not that it mattered.

But for some reason I wished to know.

I had never answered *his* question when he asked me how many I wanted.

Kids that is.

Back then, I mean.

What kind of man had he become? What kind

of husband. What kind of father? Why did I even care? It was totally irrelevant now.

I met Leo when I was sixteen. We dated through high school, and then as undergrads at the University of Toronto. Our paths diverged after he majored in animal sciences and me in plant biology. But before that we were head over heels for each other.

What would have happened had I said yes? I studied his pleasant features. He was still physically fit and he had not lost his charm. I struggled with my imagination, but the feelings were mixed.

Totally oblivious of my ramblings, Leo held Lily's head with one hand while with the other he raised the eyelid of her left eye. "What happened?" he asked. "There's some redness but it doesn't look serious. It would help if you told me the story."

I forced myself not to blush. This was the moment of truth.

I released a quiet sigh.

It all started last night, just before dinner. Charlie hadn't come home yet. I was alone in the kitchen making chili con carne, trying to decide how to season it. Before I explain further just let me interject for a moment. I dislike beans with a passion, and chilies disagree with me. I was only making this dish because it was one of Charlie's favorites. After separating the ground beef and tomato sauce mixture into two separate saucepans I emptied a drained can of kidney beans into one of them. What I would do with my portion of the sauce was eat it on top of spaghetti, while Charlie dug into his classic chili con carne with soft tortillas.

But to return to the seasoning. After tossing in a handful of oregano and parsley flakes to each pot, I added a generous dash of chili power to Charlie's. As I replaced the herbs on the spice rack, I noticed a half dozen small red-colored peppers sitting on the windowsill. Charlie had warned me that they were very hot so not to use them for anything I was cooking. He knew I reacted adversely to spicy foods. He on the other hand had the palate of a chili aficionado. The peppers were Scorpions and were one of the hottest peppers on the market. Charlie had grown them himself in patio containers. They had sat there for days, and he told me that he was drying them. After all it was winter and he refused to leave the stragglers on the vine to waste. Charlie was nothing if not economical, so he had plucked them and left them in front of the window to air dry.

Honestly, I thought I was helping when I decided to microwave them.

Little did I know what a disaster that was to prove. I sliced them in half, leaving the seeds in place, and laid them on a plate. Then I closed the appliance door and set the time.

Note to self. Fresh hot peppers cannot be microwaved.

Fresh hot peppers if microwaved can be hazardous to your health.

Leo's eyes seemed to bulge out of his head when I told him what ensued. He suppressed a laugh. He simply stared at me like I was the goofiest person he had ever met.

"Suffice to say," I concluded, "the results were unexpected. When I opened the microwave door, pepper gas came blasting out and proceeded to flood the entire house. Let me just finish by saying that my experiment with drying peppers was a big fat fail."

"Yikes," he said. And made no comment about my folly. He glanced down, uncertain of the reaction I expected, and stroked Lily's head. He made as if to examine her further. Finally, he inquired, "Any other symptoms?"

I explained about the wheezing.

To contradict me, she breathed easily. The frightening contractions while she struggled to fill her lungs last night seemed to be resolved. Her sleek chestnut and white feathers hung straight on her shiny coat. In every other way she was healthy. I just had to remember to stop feeding her so much. She was a definite foodie. Leo resisted remarking whether he agreed or not.

"What are you feeding her?" he asked.

Okay. So maybe he *had* noticed.

"Kibble mostly, but she likes fresh ground lamb. It's one of the few things that doesn't upset her stomach."

He nodded. "Well, the good news is she won't suffer any long-term effects from that little adventure. I'll prescribe a saline solution to soothe her eyes, but by tomorrow I'm sure the redness will be gone. Otherwise, she seems fine. She won't need any other medication. That wheezing was just a side effect of the pepper gas. I think it's resolved now." He finished examining Lily, and then petted her.

I nodded, giggled nervously. Confession time. Only I could pepper spray myself, *and* my fiancé's dog by trying to dry fresh hot chilies in a microwave. I spoke the sentiment out loud but Leo showed no sign that he found my comment even a little bit funny.

And then he smiled, and I remembered why I once loved him.

"Nice to see you again, Sophie," he said. "You know, we should really catch up. I'd like to know what you've been up to since we broke up. I mean other than accidentally pepper-spraying your fiancé's dog."

CHAPTER 3

I forgot all about my own vision issues and removed the sunglasses as I snorted out a chuckle.

"Oh my god, Sophie. Your eyes, they look terrible!" Leo jerked forward to examine them more closely. "You had probably best go see someone about that."

He squinted into my face as I hauled my handbag up to my chest to dig out a mirror. He was not wrong. I looked like a horror show that had stayed up too late. I appeared even worse than I had this morning when I glanced in the mirror while drying my hair.

"The pepper gas?" he inquired.

"No doubt," I answered.

"Does it sting?"

"Not too bad. Just sort of a low-level irritation. But I'm sure I'm okay. It's not affecting my vision except when my eyes tear." And just to prove it, my eyes began to water and I fetched a clean tissue from my handbag.

"I still think you should see somebody about it. It's your vision I'm concerned with. You shouldn't mess around with your eyesight. And if you don't mind my saying, Sophie, *your* eyes look much worse than Lily's."

There it was again. That feeling that I used to have when I was around him. He had always been very protective. At the time I found it stifling and somewhat annoying, but now it seemed rather endearing. Had I really changed that much? I lowered my gaze to Lily who was eager to get off the examination table, and reassured her with loving pats. Yes, I had changed; I was becoming a dog person.

My eyes met Leo's. He had been observing my interactions with Lily. He was remembering something. What?

He gave Lily a final pat and she wagged her tail. He was great with animals. That had not altered, and why would it? He had always wanted to work with animals. And I was certain he was also a great husband and father.

I suddenly felt a desire to learn more about his life.

"Hey," he said as though reading my mind. "What are you doing tonight? Want to grab a bite and catch up? My wife and kids will be out Christmas shopping. I just can't handle holiday hectic, so I was planning to get a burger or something and join up with them later. What d'you say?"

My phone suddenly rang. I excused myself for an instant and dug it out. It was Charlie. Lily was Charlie's dog and he would want a report on her condition.

I looked up at Leo. It would be rude to answer it while in the middle of a conversation but Leo nodded at me and motioned that he'd be back in a few minutes with the eye drops for Lily.

I dropped my sunglasses back over my eyes, and answered the phone. Why did I put the shades back on? It was almost like I believed Charlie could see me. And even if we were Face-timing (which we were not) and he *could* see me, he already knew I looked like hell. So—why the awkward pretense?

His voice was light. "Hi, honey. How did it go at the vet?"

"We're still here, but she's fine. The symptoms are subsiding." I lowered my voice even though Leo had left the examining room and closed the door. For some reason, I felt compelled to apologize once more. "I am so sorry, Charlie. "I did not mean to explode pepper juice all over your kitchen. I had no idea pepper gas could linger in the air like that."

Charlie had just driven up the driveway when I had run outside with Lily in my arms, coughing and wheezing, our eyes streaming with tears.

I had never felt so awful and so dimwitted in my

life.

He had been furious at first. But after an hour of airing out the house he had calmed down.

Did he still want to marry me?

I don't know.

He said yes, but I still don't know.

Opposites may attract, but can they actually live together?

He had called me 'honey' so maybe he really wasn't mad anymore.

To be truthful I cannot blame him for being angry. I had pepper-sprayed his dog.

Unintentionally of course.

"I knew she'd be okay," he said, comfortingly. "But that's not the entire reason why I called. I also wanted to let you know that I won't be home for dinner tonight. Got a mess to clear up with some suppliers. I received a delivery of mixed Christmas flowers instead of the Poinsettias that I ordered, but I shouldn't be too late. Will you be okay alone with Lily?"

"No problem," I said. If he was no longer upset with me, couldn't the order mix-up wait until tomorrow? I was tempted to ask but for fear of sounding petty I refrained from doing so.

"If you need to go out, she'll be fine on her own for a couple of hours."

I nodded, catching a flash of someone at the door. It was Leo and he indicated to me with a jab of his thumb that I should meet him at the reception desk when I was done with my call. "Thanks, Charlie. Love you. See you later."

I waited for his response but he had already disconnected.

I put my phone away and led Lily out to the front desk. Leo gave me the eye drops for Lily and reiterated instructions before he left to attend to his next patient.

"See you tonight?" he asked as he was leaving.

I nodded.

"I'll text you time and place later today."

I waved as he returned to the examining room. For some reason, as I waited for the receptionist to ring up my bill, my eye caught the poster of the black and tan Cavalier again. Rosie. Something was pulling me towards her. Why?

I wanted to know more about her background. I should have asked Leo if he had any history on her when I had the chance.

As I said earlier, I wasn't a born dog person. I had no time for dogs. But her sweet face was harkening.

The receptionist noticed my interest and raised her chin. She stopped tapping on the keyboard and rose from her chair at the computer, half stooped, to pass me the bill. "Her owners have to move out of the country for a job," she explained. "Can't take her with them." She observed my reaction as if to determine my level of commitment. "Rosie is a sweetie. She's a wonderful family dog. Good with other pets and children. In fact, she loves to wear hats and fancy collars. Actually enjoys playing dress-up."

I stepped aside and looked more closely at the photos. Beneath the main picture of her seated facing the camera was a parade of four smaller ones, each showing her wearing a different Princess Di style hat or a pair of chic sunglasses. I chuckled. "She is so adorable."

The receptionist smiled as I passed her my credit card. "They're having trouble adopting her out, mostly because of the short notice and of course because she's not a puppy. She's almost eight years old. Would you like the phone number of the owners? They need to find her a home for Christmas."

An inexplicable pang shot through me. That was three days from now. *Yes. No.*

What was happening to me? I have never thought about owning a dog.

"Um. I'll have to think about it," I said.

"Of course. But don't wait too long. She needs a new home ASAP."

CHAPTER 4

Good thing we were meeting outside on the elegant steps of the Carnegie Gallery. Couldn't let Mom see me like this. I adjusted my sunglasses and tried not to rub my eyes in the process. There would be a heck of a lot of explaining to do, and I was so tired of explaining.

Really, did I even have a rational explanation for doing what I had done?

I peered up and was struck by the hard blue sky. The sun was beginning to leak through so that gave me an excuse for the sunglasses. I parked behind the pharmacy and hurried west on foot, down King Street past the Beanermunky chocolate shop, Picone's groceries, the Horn of Plenty and Cumbrae's Meats, to the gallery. Mom was prompt as usual and already there, waiting below the steep stairs, between the white pillars of the front entrance, while I (I glanced at my phone's clock) was ten minutes late. She was dressed in beige slacks with a luxurious camel hair, wrap coat on top. Around her throat was an oversized, polka dotted cream and mushroom cashmere scarf, looped twice to rest stylishly over her chest (perhaps I inherited my sense of style from her?). We were doing some last-minute Christmas shopping. I hadn't yet found the perfect gift for Charlie. And she was looking for something special for Dad. She caught sight of me, and headed in my direction.

The Carnegie Gallery was the former home of the Dundas Public Library. It was a lovely historic building restored largely by funds provided by the Carnegie foundation. In the early 70s the building was at risk of being lost from the community due to erosion of its architectural integrity. By that I mean its foundations were crumbling. The walls were pitted and worn and the windows leaked. The roof was in dire need of replacing and the interior wanted rewiring, new plumbing and a paint job. A group of craftspeople composed of potters, shoemakers and (you'll never guess this one) a smocker rallied the local artists with the cry of: "Help artists make a living from their work!"

After a thoroughly inspected facelift, the building was declared sound and the artists moved in. The new gallery was granted charity status in 1980 and opened its doors to the public as a place to appreciate and purchase local art and crafts. From then on it was a landmark of the town.

Amelia Star, my mother, met me at the far side of the iron-caged row of three windows. I had to smile secretly when I observed her step over a crack in the sidewalk as she leaned in to kiss me. "So sorry I'm late, Mom. I had to take Lily home before meeting with you."

"You were out walking Charlie's dog?"

"Well, no. Not exactly. I had to take her to the vet for him. He's working today."

"Oh dear. I hope it's nothing serious."

"No-no. Nothing serious." I quickly diverted her before she could ask any more questions. "How's Dad? I know with the renovations you had going on, building a new sunroom; it must have driven him bonkers."

"Oh, that's all done. They finished today."

The mansion my parents lived in was built in the mid nineteen twenties. At that time sunrooms were practically non-existent. If you were a gardener and had a large property you might have a greenhouse or two to support winter plants but the trend today was to add a large glassed-in atrium if you had the space and could afford it. My mom loved plants—that is probably where I inherited the landscape architecture tendency—and her new sunroom with its high, glass ceilings could support not only a plethora of flowers and shrubs and a water feature, but also a few potted trees. Couldn't wait to see it.

"And your father is out celebrating the end of

the noise and chaos by playing golf. Now what about you? We've hardly seen you since you arrived back in town. We were both also hoping to see something of Charlie before Christmas Day." It was just like Mom to get straight to the point. Unlucky for her, this was not a point I felt like discussing at the moment.

I circled around a leaning ladder so that she wouldn't have to go under it and headed towards the steps without answering. Her remark I hoped was rhetorical and not requiring a response. As we passed by the windows, I flung a look at some posters taped to the bottom of the tall, iron-caged casements on the right side of the doors. Something familiar struck my eye. Was one of those flyers about Rosie the black and tan Cavalier up for adoption?

Mom caught the direction of my stare and said, "We used to have a dog that looked just like that when you were little."

We did? I paused. Wasn't Mom allergic?

"I don't remember that. I thought you were allergic to dogs."

Trapped in what now seemed incontrovertibly like a fib, my mom blustered, "Oh. That was ages ago. You were six years old. And I *am* allergic. Which is why we couldn't keep it." She walked past me and hurried up the steps and I followed.

"You gave it away?" I asked, grabbing her arm to force her to face me.

We were blocking the front door and some people were crowding behind us as well as in front of us trying to get in and out.

Mom jerked her arm out of my grasp and rushed ahead of me. "Come on honey, we're blocking the way."

I swung open the door and she preceded me into the gallery. It was bright inside and bustling with holiday shoppers.

"Was it a girl or a boy?" I demanded. I always wondered why my parents herded me away from any talk of dogs. I recalled asking for a dog for my tenth birthday. Because Mom was allergic, they had bought me a bike. I asked again at sixteen and that was when Dad bought me a car. They said I'd be out of the house and on my own in a few years and they would be stuck with the dog, so no dog. "What was its name?"

"It was a boy and his name was Jo Jo."

Jo Jo. Why did that not ring any bells for me? "Who named him?" I asked.

"Ah—um—you did."

Weird. I could not recall. "And he looked like Rosie?"

"Who is Rosie?" Mom asked. "Ah," she said, catching the movement of my eye that twitched towards the exit. "The adoption dog." I was reminded of the photo with Rosie in a little pink hat with a black bow and veil.

"I was thinking of adopting her," I explained,

mostly to see my mother's reaction.

"But Charlie *has* a dog."

"Lily is *Charlie's* dog. She's devoted to him. I want to bond with a dog of my own."

"But with your upcoming wedding and your big job, are you sure you have the time?"

"Why don't you want me to get a dog, Mom?"

She pushed past me deeper into the gallery towards some tables loaded with beautiful hand-blown glass and ceramic vases. "Oh, look at this, Sophie. Isn't this beautiful?" The object was a two-foot tall, hand-blown glass bird in shades of blue and white, a heron or a stork of some kind, standing on one leg with a long elegant beak. "Your father would love this. I'm going to get it for him for Christmas."

"Why don't you want me to get a dog, Mom?" I repeated.

She turned to face me. "Did I say I didn't want you to get a dog?"

Well, no. But she wasn't exactly encouraging it.

"What do you think?" she asked. "About the stork?"

"It's a heron," the volunteer behind the table corrected, affably. "Although they do look an awful lot alike." She handed my mother a card with the author's bio. "The artist is very talented. An up-and-coming local star."

"Buy it," I said.

The female volunteer glanced over at my

mother. Mom nodded. "Yes, please package this up for me."

As the woman began the arduous process of rolling the glass statuette in layers of bubble wrap and tissue paper, my mother studied my sullen expression.

The clot of shoppers had moved on. We were alone now and no one was within earshot. "What's wrong, Sophie?"

"Did I say something was wrong?" Absentmindedly I lifted my sunglasses over my hair to peer at a set of hand-blown wine goblets.

"What do you think of these, Mom? Do you think Charlie would like them?"

She looked from the glassware to me, peered closer and gasped. "Sophie, what happened to your eyes?"

Oh crap. They no longer irritated me so I had forgotten that they were still red. I guess the stress of holiday shopping, of staying with my fiancé whom I normally only spent every other weekend with and my deadline at work had me more frazzled than I realized because I suddenly burst into tears. The last straw was when I had pepper-sprayed Lily.

My mother told the cashier that she would be back in a little while to pay for her purchase, and hustled me outside, tears raining down my cheeks. Everyone was staring at us. We wove down the stairs between incoming customers, and then she walked with me down the street to an empty bench. She brushed the varnished wood free of a crust of frozen snow with a leather-gloved hand. The seat was cold but dry, and she sat me down, and then settled beside me "Now tell me what happened," she ordered.

"It was an accident," I sobbed.

Mom handed me a handful of tissues. She wrapped her arms around me as though I were a six-year-old again, and waited until I stopped blubbering. It took a little while longer than I would have liked. For some reason I had an image of myself as a little girl with my hands cupping a puppy's sweet face.

Where had that come from? The blubbering was ebbing and my thoughts were less tangled. I blew my nose and dried my eyes while my mom watched. How many times in my life had she sat with me while my eyes leaked and my emotions exploded?

I smiled weakly to reassure her that this wasn't a total meltdown. Now that that outburst had vented itself, I could talk. The constant crying wasn't helping the redeye situation any, I was sure.

Mom needed an explanation and I didn't have a better one. So here it was.

I explained once more the fiasco with the Scorpion peppers.

"Oh, honey. How could you possibly predict that that might happen? Anyone could have made that mistake."

Maybe. But you wouldn't have tried to dry them that way.

"So, that's why you had to take Charlie's dog to the vet. But all is well. She's okay, isn't she? Was Charlie upset?"

"At first, but you know Charlie. He gets over things fast."

"Yes. He's one in a million." An inner smile appeared on her face that puzzled me. She squeezed my hand. When she looked at me the expression vanished. "So, why are you still so upset? Are your eyes hurting you? Can you see all right?" Now concern was mingled with her words and I could see the worry setting in. "Look, I'll take you to the eye doctor right now."

"They can't see me until after Christmas."

"But you can't wait that long. That's five days from now." She paused and I knew what was coming. The notion had briefly crossed my mind as well. "Look, why don't you call Toby."

I shook my head. I knew why she had thought of him. She had always liked Toby. And Toby was a tried-and-true eye specialist. He would probably see me straight away for old times sake. But... How could I call Toby? Seeing two exes in one day? That would be too much.

"It looks worse than it actually is," I insisted.

"It looks terrible, Sophie."

"You should have seen me last night. My eyes

were much worse."

"Please call Toby."

I shrugged helplessly. "Okay. But I don't think Charlie will like it."

That was a lie. Charlie would be gracious—as he always was. So why had I lied?

My mother frowned. Several thoughts were tumbling about in her mind but what they were she chose to hide. She seemed unnaturally troubled because I hadn't given her any reason to believe my life was otherwise. When she spoke, her voice was cautious. "What is going on between you and Charlie?"

"Nothing. We're fine."

"Are you?" A small group of people crowded by and I refused to elaborate within earshot of strangers.

"I never understood why you and Toby broke up."

"Irreconcilable differences," I replied.

"Are you having second thoughts about Charlie? Because—"

NO.

I shook my head.

"You don't have to marry him, you know. Much as I adore him, your father and I aren't that kind of people who insist that their daughter get married just for the sake of having a husband. We only want you to get married if you love him, if he's the right man for you. And I believe—"

"He's perfect," I said.

"Good. Because I believe he's perfect too." She sat back, an expression of relief appearing on her face. "Okay then. We'll talk no more about it."

I wished I could discuss my misgivings with my mom. I wished it didn't sound so silly to my own ears. Ordinarily, I was the most grounded person on earth. But was the dream a premonition? I stared at my hand, at the one-carat diamond solitaire set in rose gold that Charlie had given to me last year.

I dared not ask my mom. To her a cracked diamond ring, even in a dream, meant something.

CHAPTER 5

Thanks to Charlie I was free to meet Leo for dinner. I neglected to mention where I was going, but then Charlie never asked, because after that conversation over the phone at the vet's, we forgot to check in again. I would see Charlie afterwards and then I would explain. It wasn't every day one met a blast from the past.

After feeding Lily her ground lamb mixed with kibble, and settling her in the living room with the TV set to a Hallmark Christmas movie, I met Leo at Betula, a casual local eatery. It was situated on King Street West near the optometrist and the dog groomer.

The shops and services that lined the road were mainly Victorian style houses refurbished to suit the business owner's needs. Their gabled roofs and tall windows were fully dressed for Christmas. Colorful winking lights surrounded the front porticos and the doors were adorned with fresh wreaths or giant red velveteen bows.

Dundas had a truly Dickensian flare about it. You half expected to see gilded horse-drawn carriages rolling down the street with men in black top hats, and women in ankle-length skirts and carrying fur muffs. In fact, on weekends during the holiday season such things did happen when horse-and-buggy rides were offered to the locals and tourists, and the carolers went out to sing in traditional period costume.

My footsteps crunched over the daytime slush that was beginning to freeze, as night closed in. The sky had a wintery purple appearance as clouds cleared to make room for the stars. I had decided to walk. Fifteen minutes in the cold air would do me good.

Leo was already seated when I entered the restaurant, nursing a beer.

He glanced up from the menu greeting me with a broad smile, as I sat opposite him. The waitress handed me a menu, cited the specials and left us alone. Leo said, grinning secretively, "Guess the Big Smoke Burger is out?"

I glanced at the item he pointed at and laughed. The sandwich came with two four-ounce patties, crisp bacon, breaded onion rings *and* pickled hot peppers.

"Yeah, no thanks," I said. "I'll take the veggie burger."

"Are you sure?" Leo asked. "It may be a falafel

patty that comes with goat cheese and arugula, but it's also accompanied by pepper mostarda. Which is a fancy way of saying pepper mustard I'm guessing."

I giggled. "You did this on purpose didn't you?"

He leaned forward and pointed to something on my menu. "Try the Southwest Crispy Blue Cod Tacos. I've had that before. It's awesome."

I read the description. *Lime crema and…* "What is pico de gallo?"

"Oh crap. I forgot. It has chilies in it too."

"I can't eat peppers. And not just because I pepper sprayed Charlie's dog." I glanced at the top of the menu. Was everything prepared with peppers at this restaurant? The restaurant was called Betula. What did Betula mean? I pulled out my phone under Leo's questioning glance and searched for a definition.

Betula was a genus of trees that included Birches. Okay, that made sense. The only food group I knew that was made from Birch trees was syrup, and good quality Birch syrup could cost an arm and a leg. Nevertheless… As long as it didn't include the family of hot peppers…

"What about old-fashioned spaghetti and meatballs?" Leo suggested. "Despite the hankering for a veggie burger, you aren't strictly a vegetarian, are you? At least you weren't when *I* knew you."

"No. But sometimes I'm in the mood for it."

I stashed away the phone and checked out the

description. Nope. No peppers.

Despite the fact that I had just eaten spaghetti the other night, when the waitress arrived, I ordered the spaghetti. Leo was unaware of that. And didn't need to be enlightened. Out of respect for me and my quarrel with hot peppers, Leo ordered the same.

After the waitress departed, he studied my face. "You look great, Sophie," he said. "You've hardly changed at all. Physically, anyways." He grinned. "Except for the ghoulish eyes. Although in this light you can hardly tell."

Yeah, yeah. They were still red.

He took a sip of his beer. "So, tell me about Charlie."

What was there to tell? I loved Charlie. He was kind and successful and level-headed. And brave. He wasn't afraid to try new things. He was altruistic to a fault. Everyone who ever met him adored him. And he never stayed upset with me even when I did stupid things. He understood how my job absorbed me and how high pressure it was. My boss was a slave driver and expected perfection. I had a lot of responsibility and my work reflected on the company, and that was why ordinary everyday life things often slipped my mind. But he never held it against me. Honest to God there were times when his kindness and understanding drove me mad. In times like that I wanted to scream. *"I don't deserve you!"*

I almost mentioned to Leo that horrible nightmare where my diamond engagement ring cracked in half. *Freudian or what?* It had to mean something.

But Leo said, "You seem to have it made. You've got everything you've ever wanted."

What do you know about what I want? When Leo and I were a couple in high school we were too young to be thinking about forever. And yet that was exactly what Leo had done. He probably already had the careers of his kids plotted out.

"Are you happy, Sophie?"

I struggled to return my attention to him.

"Yes." I hadn't hesitated with my answer and yet why did I feel like an imposter? Something was wrong, maybe not with Charlie but with me.

"You look hesitant."

I shook my head. "I'm not. I've never been so sure of anyone in my life."

"Then why do you look so confused?"

"I'm not." Okay, maybe I was.

The reason I had agreed to return to Dundas for Christmas was not just because my parents had asked me to, but also because Charlie had insisted on it. This was the first year that Mom and Dad had skipped their annual pilgrimage to Florida. Why? I don't know. Maybe as they got older, they missed the warmth and specialness of Christmas with family—and yeah, snow. As far as I was concerned you couldn't have Christmas without snow. And even though I wasn't big on Christmas, if you must have Christmas then you must have snow. Charlie felt the same. In fact, it was Christmas Eve that Charlie and I got engaged. It was snowing. And we were walking through the lightshow at the Royal Botanical Gardens, after hours, during the festival of lights. A good friend of his worked the lightshow and he had extended it as a favor to Charlie. What a romantic gesture. The trees and shrubbery like sparkling ghosts. Colorful scenes like fantasy dreams. Fantasia on steroids. How could I say no?

"Now there's the smile, I remember," Leo said, waking me up from my dreaming. "Tells me he's a keeper."

I redirected my attention to Leo as the waitress returned and set down our plates loaded with hot steamy pasta and succulent meatballs. "Oh, he is. He definitely is."

"Then what's the problem?"

"I don't know. I don't think there is a problem. Not with him anyway."

"Then…?"

I dug into my food as a way to avoid answering. He joined me. This spaghetti was so much better than anything I could make. My next comments had to do with the deliciousness of the food. It tasted like homemade, but better.

A few minutes passed as we sampled meatball after meatball, finally Leo said, "You never answered my question. If Charlie is perfect, what's the problem?"

I glanced hard at Leo. "Leo, how did you know Sloane was your happily ever after?"

His eyes teamed with amusement. "For one thing, she didn't cut and run when I mentioned that I wanted children."

I scowled good-naturedly. "I did *not* do that."

"Oh, not physically. But I knew."

"I was eighteen."

"Yes. So was I. But I already knew what I wanted. You didn't. Sloane never hesitated for an instant. She was an open book. There was no second-guessing with her."

And then, as if on cue the restaurant door swung open and two chattering kids, rosy-cheeked, a boy and a girl, eyes all aglow entered. They were around the ages of five and six respectively. The mom followed, fresh-faced and not harassed at all despite the run-about children. She was obviously pregnant and I smiled. This had to be Sloane, and David and Marilyn?

The kids came towards us, apparently recognizing Daddy's green and red plaid scarf that had remained snug around his neck all the time we were eating. I set my fork down and Leo turned to see what I was looking at.

"Daddy, Daddy!" the youthful voices screamed.

"Not so loud," Sloane chided affectionately.

The kids climbed on Leo's lap, one on either side of him. And Sloane came around and pecked him on the cheek.

"Hello," she said, turning to me. Then she noticed our almost empty plates. "Oh, forgive me. I thought you would be finished by now. We can come back." She removed her hand from her pregnant belly, and glanced at her phone. It was just after eight o'clock.

"It's okay. No point in you and the kids waiting outside in the cold. I'm finished." I glanced at Leo. He polished off the last bit of pasta on his plate and placed his fork and spoon neatly on the side of the dish.

"You must be Sophie," she said.

"I am," I replied. "And you are obviously Sloane. Unless Leo has another family he didn't tell me about."

We all laughed because they were obviously the epitome of the happy family.

For the first time in my life, I wished I had that.

She introduced the children. I was right about their names and secretly grinned. How had he convinced her to name them Marilyn and David?

The waitress came to remove our plates, asking before she left if there was anything else we required. I glanced at Leo's beautiful wife and asked if she and the kids would like dessert.

"Oh, we would have loved to, but the kids and I had ice cream at McDonalds."

My phone suddenly dinged and I excused myself to check my text. It was Charlie saying he was about to leave work and would be home soon.

"Your fiancé?" Leo said. He placed his credit card down on top of the bill the waitress had left for us.

I nodded. "He's on his way home."

"We should get going, too." He rose; hoisting David and Marilyn in either arm, then set them down in front of their mom. "I'll just pay for this, sweetheart. Meet you guys outside."

"Nice to meet you, Sophie," Sloane said. "You'll have to join us for dinner some time."

I was sure she was just being nice so I answered non-committedly. "Sure."

She smiled, a very pleasant smile. "Leo's told me all about you."

"Oh really?" I said.

"Don't worry, all nice things."

I grinned. "Thanks, Sloane."

"What are you thanking me for? *He* said them," she said teasingly. She turned back to her husband, gave him another peck on the cheek and called to the kids to follow her outside to the car. "Don't be too long, Leo. It's getting nippy outside."

"I won't."

The waitress returned just then and returned his credit card.

"Let me pay for my share," I insisted, digging in my purse for some cash.

Just like me not to have any. I never paid with cash. "Well, next time," I said sheepishly.

"Absolutely. And Sophie, don't be a stranger.

Sloane meant it when she invited you for dinner. And that includes Charlie."

I smiled. Nodded. Sloane was terribly nice. And so were the kids. And so was Leo.

We walked outside. He squeezed my hand and reminded me to give the eye drops to Lily before retiring to bed. I thanked him, said goodbye. I would have made it home earlier had I come by car. But as it was, I had a quarter hour walk—a relatively short distance—but not when you were anxious to be home.

As I reached the driveway, I saw Charlie's red pickup truck against the backdrop of his Victorian house all covered in multicolored Christmas lights. He was home. I felt a sudden surge of elation and hurried up the front porch, key already in hand.

Lily was at the door to greet me barking happily. I squatted to kiss her and pet her. "Where's Daddy?" I asked.

"In here!" Charlie's voice called from upstairs.

I unzipped my boots and left them in a puddle of melted snow. Then removed my coat, gloves and scarf and hung them on the hall hooks.

"Hey Charlie. What are you doing?" I trotted up the varnished wooden staircase with Lily at my feet to find out why he hadn't come down to greet me.

I froze as I saw the activity he was engaged in. A wash of shame overcame me.

"Oh, Charlie. I am so sorry."

"No problem, honey. I know you were in a hurry

this morning."

He was wiping up the floor that was still wet from my shower and picking up the damp towels.

You see what I mean? Sometimes I think Charlie is too good for me.

CHAPTER 6

I was mulling over unpleasant thoughts. Like why couldn't he have a glass shower like everyone else I knew? Why did he still have this old-fashioned bathtub with a plastic shower curtain that I always forgot to make sure was tucked in before I turned on the water?

He was making me feel guilty when in fact he had done nothing at all. Except clean up my mess. Maybe opposites did not attract. Maybe opposites just made life more difficult.

Charlie came to me because he could see that I was upset. But my feelings had little to do with him; I was upset with myself. I was beginning to feel like I was incapable of handling the big landscaping job —*and* our impending marriage.

He took my hand and led me out of the bathroom and into his bedroom. I looked around at the brown and green masculine furnishings. Would I ever feel like this house was mine?

Did we have to live here? Could I ask him to move to the big city?

He sat me down on the bed atop the quilted duvet. "Lily is fine. Her eyes aren't even inflamed anymore." He looked at me closely. "But *yours* are."

I shook my head. "I'm okay. Just tired."

Charlie was a tall man and his hands were large. My hand looked like a child's held by his. "Did something happen?" He paused to await my answer. Silence filled the bedroom. When I didn't answer he said, "Where *were* you tonight?"

I was out. Out with a friend. I sighed. What had I done wrong that I should feel so guilt ridden? Nothing. Nothing at all. I forced a smile. "You'll never guess."

"No." He chuckled. "I don't think I can."

"The vet, the substitute vet that examined Lily, was my ex-boyfriend Leo. Leo MacVee. You remember, I told you about him?"

He nodded. The look he gave me was tender but I could tell beneath it he was asking if he had anything to worry about.

"We're just friends," I said. "He has a wonderful wife and two gorgeous children. And another one on the way."

"Glad to hear it."

"I'm sorry I'm so moody. I think I was just overwhelmed from nearly killing your dog, and then seeing *him*. I met him for dinner tonight."

"You didn't nearly kill my dog. And she's not *my*

dog. She's your dog, too. She loves you." And to add emphasis to his statement, Lily leaped onto my lap and I swear if she was a cat she would have purred.

"How was dinner?" he asked.

"It was nice, nice to catch up. I haven't seen him since our undergrad days."

He nodded. I could tell he was at a loss for words. I could offer more details but I was uncertain if he wished me to. Staying silent however would make it appear as though I had something to hide. I did not.

On his side it was even more complicated. If he asked further questions, it would seem like he was prying. If he asked fewer it would appear like he didn't care. What exactly *did* he feel?

He brushed my hair away from my forehead. "Your eyes are still red. You should probably go see the eye doctor."

"I tried to get an appointment but the soonest they could get me in was after Christmas because it wasn't an emergency. By that time, I'm sure the inflammation will be gone."

"You don't want to go to your mom and dad's place looking like that. Your mom will have a fit."

Wrong. She had already seen me. He was right about one thing however. I was tired of looking like something out of a horror movie and needed to get it fixed. I did have another alternative. I hesitated to bring it up however. My college boyfriend Toby was an opthal—eye doctor. After we both got our postgraduate degrees, he in ophthalmology, and me in landscape architecture he had followed me back to Dundas. He found a job almost immediately right in town. I couldn't find anything local so searched farther afield. When I found my job, it was in Toronto. The plan was for us to move to the big city together, but he had fallen in love with the town and didn't want to move...

I could call him. The only thing that was stopping me was the fact that my mom had suggested it. All in all, it would be nice to learn what he'd been up to since we split up. Last I heard he was married just like Leo.

That breakup, I believe, had broken my mom's heart more than it had broken mine. It had taken her longer to recover than it had taken me.

Charlie was quiet for a long while. What was he thinking? His stare was directed towards the bathroom and I felt the guilt all over again.

He turned back to me when he noticed me studying his pensive face. He leaned forward and kissed me on the tip of my nose. "I know it's been a tough couple of months for you with this new project and your boss pressuring you, and the wedding coming up. I have an idea. Why don't you go and stay with your parents for the rest of the holidays? You clearly can't relax here, and especially not after what happened last night. Your parents' place is much nicer and way more comfortable. And you must be dying to see their new glassed-in atrium. You mentioned the work is completed now?" He grinned. "And not only will you have a marble shower stall with glass walls, but you'll also have a Jacuzzi and sauna. Can't think of anything more relaxing than that. I'll join you on Christmas Eve."

"No. I don't want to be away from you." I glommed onto his arm.

"It will only be for two days. And maybe being away from me is what you need."

No. I don't think so. But I kept seeing his pensive face, even though he had managed to disguise it with a cheerful mood. "I insist," he said. "You need a break, and maybe some mother-daughter time."

He seemed quite urgent and sincere about the idea.

Was being away from me what *he* needed?

CHAPTER 7

The next day after Charlie left for work, I called Toby's office. He was listed as Dr. Toby Jerome MD FRCSC MSc. Don't ask me what all those letters meant. I recognized the MD and the MSc, but the letters in between were like mulligatawny soup.

I spent the next fifteen minutes imagining what it might be like to have been married to an omphth—an *oph*thalmologist. I could never pronounce that word without tripping on my tongue.

I conjured up annual Christmas parties with stuffed-shirt doctors discussing detached retinas, macula degeneration and cirrhosis of the liver (the latter from consuming too much alcohol, not anything to do with the eyes) and other unpleasant things. Toby would have insisted we limit our offerings of alcohol to beer, wine and cider.

I phoned Dr. Jerome's office and asked to speak

to him directly. I informed the receptionist that I was an old friend and would wait for him to return my call. I wasn't sure that he would, at least not so soon, as specialists in his field were exceptionally busy.

But he *did* phone. About an hour after I disconnected the call.

I told him what the problem was and assured him it was probably nothing, but that my fiancé *and* my mother insisted that someone examine my eyes.

"Congratulations," he said. "Who's the lucky fella?" catching the reference to a fiancé.

I hardly wished to waste his time catching up over the phone so I said, "*I'm* the lucky one," and he laughed.

Time seemed to compress as we joked around. It was like only days had passed since we last talked —instead of five years. He suggested that I time my arrival for approximately two hours from now. He was on lunch break then. From what I'd described of my symptoms he figured the examination would only take minutes.

I texted Charlie that I had an appointment, and he texted back: "Great."

When I messaged him who the doctor was, I met with dead space.

Had he been called away by a customer? Or was he troubled by the fact that I was about to reunite with yet another ex-boyfriend. Charlie wasn't the jealous type as far as I knew. But there was always a first time for everything.

I arrived promptly at a very modern office block. His office was on the ground floor. After seeing this place, I could understand why he never wanted to move from here. It was very small-town chic, with all the amenities of the city and none of the hustle and bustle, and hassle. The waiting area was tastefully decorated with what appeared to be a fresh coat of cool, gray paint on the walls, and white accenting the trim. The seats were non-conventional. He actually had comfortable upholstered sofas and armchairs in dark gray with polished light-colored wood frames. Magazines like *Time*, *Maclean's*, and *National Geographic* were fanned neatly across the matching coffee tables.

The waiting area was busy. The officious receptionist informed me of a half-hour wait, before the doctor could see me. To kill time, I perused some news items on my phone, but I was really just mindlessly scrolling up and down as, I noticed, was everyone else seated around me. Finally, I closed my phone and picked up a magazine. I fared no better with the print news. I flipped the magazine from front to back then back to front, words landing in my sight then jumping out again. I don't believe I retained one single bite of information from what I read.

Toby himself came out to get me eventually. We greeted each other like doctor and patient but once the door closed behind us, inside his private office, we exchanged tentative hugs. It was kind of strange.

He looked good. Middle height. Still slim. How did I appear to him? I wondered. Leo had said I looked the same. Did Toby agree?

He was looking but made no comment.

He indicated a comfortable-looking leather chair opposite his desk. I sat down and glanced around. The décor of the room was simple but smart. The colors were muted—taupe, white and mahogany. His desk was clean of any clutter. Except for a tidy stack of files and a computer, there were only two other things on its surface—a neat potted winter fern and a framed photograph. His diplomas hung on the wall in dark brown frames. Wow, I had no idea he had so many. The lighting came from circular recesses in the ceiling. It was bright.

I removed my sunglasses before he even asked.

"I see what you mean," he said, raising my chin. He lifted my right eyelid and examined my sclera. Ordinarily they were whiter than white, with the help of a little Visine. But I hadn't dared use any over-the-counter eye drops in case it made the condition worse.

"How long has it been like this?" he asked.

"A day and a half."

"Any blurring of vision?"

"No," I answered.

"Any pain?"

"Not any more."

He sat back against his desk and smiled at me. "Don't worry, Sophie. It's nothing serious. Your blood vessels are dilated by an irritant. The redness will diminish certainly by tomorrow. I can give you some soothing eye drops, but you won't need any prescription medication."

The initial awkwardness had passed. True it was weird to be examined by one of your ex-boyfriends, but it was even weirder that we hadn't seen each other in almost half a decade. "Thanks, Toby," I said. "You have no idea how relieved I am."

"Just don't rub them."

He was about to get up to fetch me the eye drops when he stopped and swung back. "So, what happened? How *did* you get your eyes so inflamed?"

Naturally he was going to ask. I sighed. *Here I go again.* I smiled weakly at him. "You're going to think this is really funny."

"Well—if it has to do with you, I probably will."

"Don't laugh." If there was one thing I remembered about Toby, it was that he had a terrific sense of humor.

"No promises," he said.

"You don't really need to know, do you? It's not a medical requirement?"

"If you want my diagnosis to be accurate, I probably should know."

Rats.

So here was the story. Round two. I told him

about the whole pepper fiasco. I described in detail how I had opened the microwave door and pepper gas had sprayed me in the face. And then how the hot chili fumes, now airborne escaped throughout the kitchen to invade every corner of the house. I had grabbed Lily and raced upstairs to avoid the peppery gas, both of us wheezing and coughing and eyes streaming tears, only for me to lock Lily in the bathroom with the windows wide open and race back down to throw open every conceivable obstacle to full ventilation on the main floor—in the middle of winter. That meant every single door and window.

The pepper gas refused to dissipate and I grabbed a scarf from the coat hooks in the front hall to wrap up my nose and mouth, rushed back up the stairs to locate Lily in the bathroom, scooped her up and stumbled back downstairs and out the front door, snagging my winter jacket as we flashed by.

It was then Charlie pulled up in his red pickup truck.

Toby was practically on the floor laughing.

In retrospect it was pretty hilarious. It was like the scene out of an early Jim Carrey movie. At the time however it was not funny at all. I was petrified that I had permanently injured Charlie's sweet dog.

"Stop laughing," I said. "You promised."

He removed his glasses and wiped a tear from his cheek. "I did nothing of the sort."

"I guess from your perspective it *is* rather

comical."

"Rather?" He snorted. "Sophie. That just doesn't happen in real life!"

"Yes, it does. It happened to me." I giggled nervously. If it hadn't been for my worry over Lily I probably would have been laughing hysterically too.

But Charlie had not found it funny.

Certainly not at first.

"The dog's okay?"

I nodded. "She's fine. I took her to the vet yesterday."

I happened to glance at the framed photograph that had been knocked askew when Toby was so thoroughly enjoying my mortification. It was a picture of Toby with a stylish woman and a toddler, and a dog. The dog I recognized.

"Toby," I said, righting the photo and pointing. "Is that your dog?"

He chuckled. "Only you would notice the pooch first. But yes—you guessed it—that's my dog. And that's Aliisa, my wife, and our three-year-old son Karl."

I reached for the photo, tilted my eyes up and said apologetically, "So sorry. I *did* notice your family first. They're beautiful. Of course, they are. But the dog—is her name, by any chance, Rosie?"

CHAPTER 8

His jaw dropped just a tad. He stared at me as though I were some kind of psychic. Then the puzzled expression vanished, and he smiled. "Oh, I get it. You saw the posters I have around town."

I nodded. "So, you're moving? Where to? And why?" The questions had just slipped out before I realized I had spoken. The answers, if he chose to provide them, were none of my business, but it was impossible to retract the fact that I had asked.

His eyes gleamed with humor. Typical Toby. It was a familiar reaction and gave me courage, setting me at ease. He was the type of individual that was difficult to offend. That was why he made a great doctor. He had an effective bedside manner. *Calling all reluctant, nervous or cranky patients—Dr. Toby Jerome is in the office.* Other folks would just become frustrated or exasperated. Not Toby. He knew exactly how to diffuse an awkward situation.

It was done with humor.

And yet, it was one thing to connect with people; it was another thing to meddle. Toby seemed not to mind my directness. After all, we were hardly strangers. "Who told you I was moving?" he asked gently.

"The receptionist at the Spencer Creek Animal Hospital."

"Ah. Well, it's true. My wife, Aliisa is Finnish and her family lives in a town outside of Helsinki. It's a large town and has need of our services. Aliisa is an obstetrician, did I tell you? We have jobs waiting for us there. Sadly, her father is dying from a rare degenerative disease, and wants to spend as much time with his grandson as possible. When he's gone, her mother will be alone. Aliisa doesn't want to leave her alone in Finland but she refuses to consider a move here."

"Wow. That's huge of you, Toby. I know how much you love Dundas."

"I love my family more."

I didn't want to inject any personal meaning into that statement. Had I been in a self-pitying mood I might have. If you recall, back in the day, he had been reluctant to move for *me*. That fact was irrelevant to this situation however. "And you can't take the dog?" I inquired politely.

He shook his head. "We love Rosie. But I don't think she would enjoy the journey. It's Finland. Besides, Dundas is her home. She was born and raised here. Everything that is familiar to her is here. I'm hoping to find someone local to adopt her."

He smiled mischievously not ever knowing me to have a dog. "You interested?"

I returned an impish curl of the lips. "Well... Sort of."

His eyes widened. Was he getting excited? Oh-oh.... "Seriously? Please don't be joking, Sophie. I need to find Rosie a home." He paused. He seemed to do some rapid assessment inside his head. He pushed himself off, away from his desk with one hand, and leaped to his feet. "Wait here. I want you to meet someone."

He hurried over to a closed door and opened it. The sounds of a man greeting his best friend came in a rush of excited barks and scuffling nails. I could see that the dog had been confined to Toby's personal bathroom. She came scrambling out chasing a babble ball. The ball was one of those battery-operated toys that responded to the vibrations or even the breath of a dog. And look out if you rolled it. It talked. "Ouch, don't do that!" it squawked.

Although I knew what to expect—I had seen her pictures—the sense of familiarity rocked my senses. I was filled with an odd sensation of joy and fear, mixed with a generous dollop of confusion. I was beginning to regret having spoken.

"We already have *one* dog—" I stuttered.

"We?" Toby asked, looking up from playing with his dog.

"Yes, me and Charlie. My fiancé. Remember?" I removed my gray leather glove, stuck out my hand to flaunt the white diamond solitaire in its rose-gold setting when I realized it had spun around to palm-side. I corrected it.

Toby tossed the talking ball and Rosie ran after it. She swatted it with her paw and retrieved it in her mouth. The ball made giggle sounds and said, "Yeah, baby."

Meanwhile Toby approached me where I leaned forward in the comfy chair. He stooped down and gave me a very genuine bear hug. Rosie ran over and gave me a genuine swish-swish of the tail.

"Oh geez, I thought you were kidding. Congrats, Sophie. I am so happy for you."

Why would he have thought that I was kidding? Marriage as far as I was concerned was not a thing to take lightly. I squeezed him back. "Thanks, Toby."

"When's the big day? Am I invited?"

Always straight to the point, was Toby. His face was deadpan but a glimmer in his eyes made me realize he was mocking me. He was hardly going to fly back from Finland to attend my wedding.

I laughed in his face, accepting the challenge. "Early June. Will you come?"

He lowered his eyes and sent me a teasingly, demure look. "I am tempted. I would really like to meet this guy. Tell you what. Aliisa and I are giving ourselves a going-away shindig on Christmas Eve. It'll just be some friends and neighbors and work colleagues. I'd love for you to meet her. Why don't you and Charlie come?"

I stared at him speechless. Less than an hour ago Toby Jerome was part of my past. Even though we lived within travelling distance of each other—me in Toronto, he here in Dundas—we had drifted apart. It had never occurred to me to get in touch with him after our breakup. What was his motive for inviting me? *Did* he have a motive? Toby was an eye doctor; his wife was a baby doctor. *Did* it get any more perfect than that? Did he want to flaunt his spectacular life in my face or was he just being nice?

And then I realized Toby wasn't like that. He wasn't a social climber. He could give two hoots about what the Joneses were up to. He didn't even have an Instagram page, a Facebook page or a Twitter account. I know—because I checked.

"What about it, Soph?" He used to call me Soph. Only *he* ever called me Soph.

"I'll ask Charlie."

"Please do that. I'd really like you to come. Meanwhile" —he glanced down affectionately— "there's still the issue of Rosie."

The black and tan Cavalier was right at my feet with the ball. I leaned over from where I still sat in the chair to pat her. She raised her paws onto my lap, long curly black ears dangling, and hung out her tongue. I swear she was smiling.

She was adorable. But that feeling of caution that had struck me when I saw the framed photo on Toby's desk returned full force now. I used my full wits to keep from recoiling.

"She's as friendly as anything," he said. It wasn't that I was afraid of her.

I yanked my head up and then down, as he dropped to a squat beside me to officially introduce us. "Rosie? Meet Sophie Star. Sophie, this is Rosie."

He scratched the pup behind the ears. I could see he was attached to her and that surrendering her to a new owner would be hard. He wanted it to be me because he was well acquainted with my temperament and my personal habits. My conscientiousness and kindness suited him. I know —because he had once told me so. And he knew that she would be well cared for and loved in our home.

But at the moment I felt scared. Absurdly scared.

And yet there was nothing remotely terrifying about this dog.

My hands had gone ice cold. My breath was shallow.

"Sophie," Toby said. I felt my name echoing in my head. "Soph? Sophie?" The sound was getting more and more faint. The dog's paws were touching the bare skin of my wrists. I suddenly stood up and her upper torso slid off my knees and thumped to the ground.

"Sophie?" Toby rose from Rosie's side to grip my

shoulders. I swayed a little, standing on unsteady feet, then felt my vision settle. Toby who was half a head taller than me (with my boots on) waved a finger in front of my eyes. "Sophie, are you alright?"

I took two deep breaths, giggled nervously. "Am I supposed to be seeing one finger or two?"

"How many do you see?"

"One."

He nodded. "That's all you're supposed to see."

My face had gone pallid but the color was returning to my cheeks. I felt flushed.

"What happened?" he asked.

"Nothing that hasn't happened before." Not entirely true, but hopefully he wouldn't question it.

Rosie had scrambled away after the ball that moved of its own accord. "Hot diggity dog," it said. The pup was okay. I wasn't totally sure that *I* was.

"I was wondering if maybe you don't have an ear thing going on there. Sometimes trapped water from your shower can cause that momentary dizzy sensation."

"Yes, that's probably all it was. I'm fine."

Toby released my shoulder. "Got any ex-boyfriends that are ear, throat and nose specialists?" That was supposed to be a joke.

I laughed.

He suddenly noticed that my coat was disheveled. The belt had unloosened and hung sloppily to one side. I tightened it. One explanation for my odd behavior was the obvious: I was not dressed for doggy playtime.

"Sophie, I am so sorry. I shouldn't have let her climb all over your nice outfit like that. Did she mark your coat? I'll have it dry cleaned."

"No. No," I uttered quickly. "No, please. It wasn't Rosie. I—I just had a bout of vertigo. Happens sometimes when I move my head too fast. It's passed now. I'm sorry… I'm okay." I lowered myself to my haunches to reassure Toby and his dog that I was fine. Rosie brought the ball to me. When she dropped it, the ball squeaked: "Ouch, don't do that!"

I could feel Toby staring at the top of my head, as he stood there, torn between his occupation as doctor, his past role as boyfriend and this current casual reunion. I tipped my gaze up towards him as I crouched next to Rosie, and said, "I'm fine, Toby. Honestly."

His nod was hesitant but he knew better than to pursue it. As I rose, he held out his hands. "Well, before you go…." He studied me in an attempt to gauge my mind. "You were about to tell me about the dog you currently have—before I brought Rosie out to meet you."

I paused for a moment to compose myself. "Ah, well, she's not really mine. She belongs to my fiancé. But I adore her."

"That's great because I'd really love it if you were serious about adopting Rosie. She gets along well with other pets." He was speaking quickly now in an attempt to prevent me from changing my mind. "Maybe you could bring Charlie's dog to meet her? Or we could meet somewhere neutral like a park or in the forest trail—with Charlie's okay of course. What is her name?"

"Lily."

"That's a pretty name. What breed is she?"

"She's a Cavalier just like Rosie. Only she's a Blenheim."

"A Cavalier. Terrific. Same breed. That practically guarantees they'll get along." Toby's enthusiasm was infectious. He was totally oblivious to the fact that a moment ago I was poised to go racing out of the room in the midst of a full-blown panic attack. "Rosie, precious. Come to Papa." He hefted her into his arms and raised her to my eye level."

"Hello sweetie," I said nervously.

"She likes you," he said. He indicated the swishing tail that was hanging from between his elbows and brushing his thighs.

Against my better judgment I promised to meet with him. But first I had to tell Charlie about Rosie. Maybe he could give me an idea as to why I felt the way I did around her. If he was on board—and I had no doubt that he would be—we could get the dogs together to see how they took to one another. If I saw them together, I might get some insight into why she had this strange effect on me.

Toby gave me a free sample of some OTC eye drops, no prescription necessary. He helped me to apply two drops to each eye and then we said our goodbyes.

The plan was to meet at the gardening center tomorrow.

CHAPTER 9

I moved to my folks' place that afternoon. Somehow Charlie had convinced me that it was a good idea. It just made sense, since we would be spending Christmas with them anyway. And after what happened at Toby's office... Well, maybe he was right and I needed a change of scenery and a place where I could seriously relax. Besides, there was something I wished to discuss with my mom. Charlie promised he would join us as soon as he was able.

The folks were out when I arrived. More shopping I supposed. Mom had left a note on the kitchen counter, which I didn't pay much attention to.

Something about a check for the contractor.

I was about to go upstairs when I heard a phone ring. It wasn't the landline. The telltale chime was typical of an iPhone. Had Toby forgotten to tell me something about my eyes? I patted my pockets fruitlessly. My phone was upstairs on my dresser inside my handbag, so it wasn't mine that was ringing.

The source of the incessant chime was on the counter by the stove. It was my mom's phone. Oh boy, would she be annoyed when she realized she had forgotten it.

I scooped it up but it had already gone to voicemail. On the screen was the message:

Charlie Payne. Missed call.

Curious. Why was Charlie phoning my mom? Had he tried to reach me and then called her? I ran upstairs to dig out my phone. No. No missed call from Charlie. No voicemail. No text either.

Well, the folks wouldn't be home for hours. When they went out, they usually made a day of it. I decided to unpack.

My old bedroom had been rejuvenated somewhat since my teen days. The walls were painted a pale mint-green, replacing the baby pink I used to love. The trim remained spanking white and appeared to have been given a recent fresh coat of paint. Seemed like everyone in town had leaped aboard the renovation train this year.

The duvet and multiple pillow covers were of mint green, yellow and crisp white. And there were three accent cushions fanned across the head of the bed in bright turquoise for contrast. The bay windows had tiny potted daisies on the satin white windowsill interspersed with silvery green Frosty Ferns. Now, how had Mom managed to find live daisies in the middle of winter?

It was while I was hanging my dresses in the walk-in closet that I heard a knock on the door. I waited a few seconds to make sure I had heard right before I hurried down the left side of the double princess stairway, under the crystal chandelier, to the front foyer. In the mirror over the lacquered chest, I scrutinized my appearance: hair kind of flyaway, but the eyes were almost normal, ever so slightly pink, but nothing a stranger would comment on. The drops that Toby had administered were already working.

I smoothed down the chestnut wisps, and before I even reached the door, I noticed through one of the clear, floor-to-ceiling, oblong windows flanking the double doors, a large, familiar black truck. What was that humongous thing doing parked in the circular drive outside my parents' house?

This time the doorbell rang. I composed myself, patted my designer jeans and tugged at my white, cowl-neck cashmere sweater. I crossed the remaining marble tiles, and opened the right side of the double doors.

My heart virtually stopped when I saw who was standing there. Although that preliminary glimpse outside should have prepared me for his presence, I was still caught off guard. My ex. *No, I don't mean*

Toby. Or Leo. It was ex number three.

It was probably only a few seconds, but the stunned silence that greeted us both seemed to last for ages.

I recovered first. "Abe? What are you doing here?"

"Hi, Sophie." He behaved just as uneasy as I felt. His face had colored slightly and his muscular build was stiff. "Your parents told me you were back in town."

They did? Then why didn't they mention they had hired Abe as their contractor? That was the reason he was here, wasn't it? Or had my parents become buddy-buddy with another one of my former boyfriends?

No, that wasn't it. The age gap was too wide. What could they possibly have in common? Why would they be friends? The logical explanation was that Abe was their contractor. My head swung sharply, my eye briefly shot past the staircase to the sunlit atrium. They had every right to hire him and he to accept the job. So, why not tell me? Enough of the jibber jabber monologue. Abe was waiting. My head jerked back to the familiar man in the doorway.

Or maybe they had mentioned it to me, and the news had washed in one ear and out the other. These days I had a real sieve brain. But surely, I would have remembered? Well, well, well. *Three times a charm.* Now why had *that* phrase popped into my head? The saying wasn't even appropriate. Just because in the last three days I had been reunited with my exes—the three most important men in my life prior to Charlie—did *not* mean beans.

But oh my gosh. This contractor was the last person I had had a serious relationship with before I met Charlie. That was at least a couple of years ago. My company had hired Abe's firm (which he owned), to build an outdoor kitchen, dining and living room that I had designed for one of my clients. Somehow, we had clicked. However, the clicking did not last. Eighteen months later he asked me to marry him. Why I gave his proposal a hard pass is beyond me. Abe is wealthy, successful, talented and a decent human being. There was nothing very much wrong with him, and everything very much right.

It was me. It *had* to be me. And I was getting cold feet again. With Charlie.

"I heard you're getting married," he said.

Scenes from the movie *Runaway Bride* stampeded through my brain. I was no actress. Oh sure, I did a little bit of drama club in high school. But I was certainly nothing like Julia Roberts. I did not wish to discuss my future nuptials. I still felt bad about turning Abe down. Of the three men in my past, I felt the worst about Abe. Leo had been a teenage thing—puppy love. There were no hard feelings. My relationship with Toby had been more mature, but we were just starting out in our careers. He wanted one thing; I wanted another. We had both agreed we had no future together. But Abe. There was no reason a life with Abe should not work out. We had so many things in common, namely building outdoor spaces. We also liked the same kind of food, books, music and movies. When off the clock he drove a Porsche, not a pickup truck. His house was ultra modern like my condo. He had a glassed-in shower.

Our split up was also relatively fresh.

Abe's deep voice cut into my thoughts. "Congrats on the engagement. I just dropped by to see your mother. She said she had a check for me."

He did not seem resentful or even particularly interested in my life.

"Of course, that's right," I said, looking up at him. "She told me that her contractor was coming by for final payment, but I had no idea it was you."

"Probably because I changed the name of my company."

"You did?"

"Yeah. I wanted to rename it after my daughter."

I swallowed. "You... have a daughter?" After less than three years he already had a family?

He nodded. "Fresh start. She is just over a year old and her name is Dominique, hence the name of my company." He shoved a stylish business card into my face.

"I—I had no idea you had gotten married," I stammered.

"I'm not married. Yet. We plan to tie the knot this summer."

"Oh wow. I'm so happy for you, Abe. What does she do?"

"She's an interior designer," he replied. "We met on a job."

Oh my. The same way Abe and I had met. On a job.

"Does my mother know?" I hoped I was not being too nosy. I must ask her when she got home why she had kept her business with Abe a secret. I was feeling a little overwhelmed. What were the odds of being reunited with three of my exes in one week? My emotions were in overdrive: too much to think about; too many past relationships to analyze. Why was I even analyzing them? Overwhelmed was an understatement. And why did it sting to hear that Abe was getting married?

I tried to squash down the storm of thoughts and questions. The best way out of the cacophony was to repeat my question: "Does my mom know? I would have thought she might have told me."

"No. It's not public yet." He smiled. "Whereas, I hear *your* engagement is."

I didn't know what else to say. I was stymied. How did he know that I was getting married? Had Mom told him? Why would she tell him? He was her contractor. Since when did mothers have tête-à-têtes with their contractors? And why hadn't she informed me of the hiring? (I know I sound like a defective CD—why-oh-why-oh-why had she hired my ex?) Did she not remember that Abe and I had dated for over a year and a half? And that he had proposed?

I was about to ask him how he knew my mother, but then I realized I had introduced him to my folks when we were getting serious. And of course, I had run to them when my life with Abe fell apart. So yes, she knew him. Was that why she had chosen him to build her sunroom—other than the fact that he had a superlative reputation in the industry?

His gaze flitted towards the new sunroom that opened out from the kitchen and onto the flagstone patio. You could only catch a glimpse of the tall glass panels past the left side of the princess staircase from where we chatted at the front door.

A rush of winter wind blew past me into the house. It dawned on me with the weight of a brick that my manners were lacking. We had been standing here for nearly ten minutes, playing catch-up.

CHAPTER 10

"Come inside. I'll get your check. Mom left it on the kitchen island."

I was swarmed with thoughts and feelings inappropriate for me to have, considering we were no longer an item or even friends. That however was no excuse for my behavior. How boorish of me. I should have invited him in the moment I confirmed his identity.

He closed the door. I indicated that he should follow me across the marble foyer to the recently updated kitchen. Like any good contractor he was considerate of the homeowner's property and bent down to unlace his boots. I waited as he got them off. Then he carried the boots one-handed and followed.

At the dusty rose quartz island, I plucked a check from its sparkling surface. One glance at the company logo told me it was for him.

Dominique.

It was a lovely name.

"So, what do you think?" he asked after accepting the payment with his free hand. He was pointing with the check at the huge, glass domed atrium that opened off the kitchen. "I'm just going to take a final look around. Want to join me?"

I trailed after him, both of us in stocking feet, drawn by the sound of falling water. There was an enormous, functioning stone fountain surrounded by Italian tiles, where pots of ivies, ferns and other water-loving plants thrived. Several dark green palms, stiff-leafed fig trees and scarlet poinsettia shrubs provided shade. UV protective glass blocked the sun's rays, sending rainbows of light onto the up-reaching plants. At the patio doors Abe placed his boots on a drying mat.

The space was stunning, something you would have expected to see in a national botanical garden. "I always said you do magnificent work," I commented generously.

"Thanks. So do you."

I smiled. *We used to work together, and now we don't.*

I was quiet for several minutes as Abe studied his handiwork. The tile floors and recessed lighting were newly installed, the plants fresh, vital and healthy. No sign of the workmen remained. They had cleaned up diligently and removed all of their equipment and tools, leaving the new atrium spotless and pristine. When he turned back to me, I was gazing blankly at the fountain.

He was talking—about what I have no clue—my mind was distracted. It might even have been the fountain making that rhythmic murmuring sound I thought was his voice. And then it stopped. I think it was the silence that brought me back to the present.

"I recognize that look," he said. "What's on your mind?"

"Nothing," I replied. Many, many things were on my mind. I cannot tell you how overwhelmed I was. I couldn't even begin to explain. The burbling of water resumed and fell loud in my ears. "I—I was just startled to see you, I guess."

"Sorry."

I turned to face him. My brain was fit to explode. I had to get my feelings out. It was long overdue. "No. *I'm* sorry. I owe you a huge apology, Abe."

I had run out on him the night he proposed. I had up and run, taken an Uber to my parent's mansion to hide. Who *did* that!

He had made the special trip from Toronto, even though it was out of the way (an hours drive for God's sake), to take me to my favorite place. It was Quatrefoil one of Dundas' premiere restaurants. That place was elegant with white table linens and fine cloth napkins, and sconces on the walls that emitted a soft romantic light. While my head was turned, he had placed the ring on an edible violet on top of my vanilla soufflé dessert, next to a single lit candle.

"You owe me an apology? Whatever for?" he prodded.

By the look on his face, I was certain he knew. And when I glanced at Charlie's diamond on my hand his head bobbed intelligibly. He was being kind to spare my feelings. He would have preferred to just forget the whole incident had ever happened. But my conscience prevented me from doing so. The edges of his mouth twitched. "It's all ancient history, Sophie. I knew I was taking a chance when I impulsively popped the question. I should have clued in that you weren't ready. I just wish I had had the sense to make it more private." His frown broke into a smile and he said, "Seriously, Sophie. You can't feel bad about that."

But I do. He had no idea how long it had haunted me.

"I was scared," I tried to explain. "And I don't know why."

He nodded, gently touched my shoulder. The gesture indicated that there was no need to elaborate. He understood. "Getting hitched, for us, probably wasn't the best idea. I'll admit I was pretty upset when you ran out of the restaurant like that. But I've had time to think since then. It was a bad idea. On reflection, I know it was. You had some things to work out. So did I. I hope you worked them out?"

That makes two of us. But it seemed I hadn't worked anything out. And he had.

"I'm happy, Sophie. And I would think that you are too. You're getting married. Why so glum?"

I shook my head. Admittedly I had pulled a long face. "I'm not sad. I just feel like something is missing."

"In your relationship?"

"No. Charlie is perfect. Before I met Charlie, I felt like I had been waiting at a bus stop all of my life."

A hard silence crashed between us. The gurgle of the fountain accelerated.

Good grief. What must that sound like! What must Abe think? Anyone, and I mean *anyone,* might interpret that statement adversely. Talk about having no filters. I was usually the coffee queen, that's how carefully I normally chose my words. Filter tight.

I was stressing out and stuff was just spilling out of my mouth.

It was no reflection on him. He was great. I must explain. I had hurt him once before; I refused to blunder again.

I hurriedly rushed in with a counter explanation. "I didn't mean it to sound like you were a waste of my time. Oh no. I didn't mean that at all, Abe."

My arms were flapping like a fledgling bird in my flustered state. I reined in my comical muscle spasms and clapped my arms across my chest. It was impossible for me to explain what I was driving at. It was as though there was a hole in my memory. And when I said that *'something was missing'* I meant it literally. And by my comment: *'Before I met Charlie, I felt like I had been waiting at a bus stop all of my life'* I merely meant that I was still waiting for that gap to fill in. Then I would feel complete. Because, you know, the last time I took a bus was probably never. My parents were overprotective. They objected to the idea of young teens taking public transit by themselves. By the time I reached driving age I had a car.

Babbling again. *Like the fountain.*

He smiled. "No apologies necessary, Sophie. There was a reason you didn't want to marry me. Have you figured out why?"

When I failed to answer he bailed me out. "It was for the best—because if you hadn't dumped me, I might have dumped you. Eventually I would have met Kate and then things would have gotten *really* messy. As it was, things turned out astonishingly well. If you hadn't ended it, I would not have Dominique. *She* turned my life around."

What did he mean? Why did he need to have his life turned around? I stared saucer-eyed at him. "There was nothing wrong with your life."

He shrugged. His hands flipped in the air. "Oh,

I was successful in a manner of speaking, but I felt like you. Like I was going nowhere."

I gave him a limp smile. "We had so much in common."

"That doesn't always make for the best match."

I disagreed. "Charlie and I are so different. Half the time we can't even eat the same foods."

"So what? Maybe you should focus on the things you *do* have in common, and *not* on the things that you don't."

I squeezed his arm. "When did you get so smart?"

"Oh, I was *always* smart. You just never noticed."

I sent my gaze around the semi-circular space to admire his craftsmanship. The atrium really was exquisite, and so serene. The entire room was filled with plants and the sun filtered through the foliage of the taller ones giving the sense of being in a manmade jungle. Mom had chosen all of these plants herself. And I realized she and Abe must have worked very closely together. For months. Where was I all that time?

The short answer? Too busy to notice.

Most of the plants were tropical. In the center of the atrium was a sitting area with cast iron sofas and armchairs, their frames painted white, and with upholstered seat cushions in turquoise and tangerine, and matching accent pillows. There was a long white, cast-iron coffee table decorated with a glass bowl of green apples, as well as several end tables. A tall white, triple bookcase behind the sitting area was filled with hardcover books, mostly about gardening and interior design.

"Amelia has good taste," Abe said, using my mom's first name. He was still fingering the check and now he stuffed the check in his wallet and put it away. "Well, it was nice seeing you again. I wish you the best, Sophie."

He turned to leave, and then pivoted back. "Oh, I forgot to tell Amelia about something. He went over to the bookcase and reached up to the top to bring something to eye level. "When we were excavating the floor of what used to be part of the backyard, before pouring the concrete foundation for the tiles, one of the workmen found this—"

"What is it?" I took it from him and spun it slowly in my hands.

He shrugged. "It was buried about three feet deep in the ground."

It looked like a tiny silver cremation urn, about six inches tall and four inches wide. It was sealed and wrapped in plastic.

"It was buried?" I frowned.

He nodded. "Don't know how long it's been down there. The plastic has not deteriorated at all, and whatever that thing is inside looks in good shape."

He watched me muse over the strange object a few more moments, and then he leaned in and kissed me on the cheek. "Sorry I can't be more helpful. But I'd best get going. Any ideas what it is?"

I shook my head.

"Anyways, it was dug up early in the project and put aside. The guys forgot about it until a couple of days ago. One of them brought it to me yesterday. I left it in here in case it was something your folks wanted, but I forgot to mention it the last time I saw them—which I believe was also yesterday. So, can you let them know about it? And thank them for the payment. I'll be in touch. If there are any deficiencies tell Amelia to call me. I start work on a new job tomorrow. But I'll be within reach."

"Sure, thanks," I said.

He didn't touch me again. He paused and he was watching me. Some thoughts were thundering about in his head but I had no idea what they were. Nor was I entitled to know. He tugged on his boots and laced them, and then he turned towards the exit. He zipped up his hoodless black parka, which he had not removed all the time we were inside, and stepped onto the patio.

I slipped on a pair of Mom's outdoor slippers that were at the side of the mat. I followed him out the double-paned doors, admiring the heavy, white latticework over the glass. The exit led from the atrium to the pink, stone patio terrace where some of the summer's potted plants had turned coppery silver from the cold. The snow removal people had been by and the terrace was free of snow except for a small clump here and there that had been missed. Tall sweeping conifers raked the deep sky and gray-edged clouds scudded past. He had already given me my parting kiss, which I barely noticed. We smiled at one another one more time, and then I watched him saunter down the cleared steps to the clean flagstone walkway.

He turned back to face me, and raised a hand before taking the right-hand path to the front of the house where his truck was parked.

"Bye, Abe."

My voice was merely a whisper as I returned his wave, but his back had already disappeared around the corner.

Commitment was a serious thing. I hoped this time I had got it right.

I pivoted on my heel, and walked back indoors.

CHAPTER 11

The plastic wrapped urn sat on the coffee table where we had left it. I picked it up and turned it over between my fingertips. Whoever had discovered it had done a good job of brushing off the soil. It was very clean except for a cloudy appearance to the plastic. What was this thing? Was it truly an urn? Who or what did it contain, and why was it buried in the backyard? And why did I find it so mesmerizing?

If it really was a cremation urn why not scatter the ashes and display the urn indoors?

Mom and Dad, what are you hiding?

Holding it gave me a strange feeling. Not the willies exactly. Because I realized this couldn't be an urn to hold a human being—it was much too small. But I had a surreal feeling similar to the dream I had experienced with the cracked diamond. As though this thing—whatever it represented—was critical to my happiness, even though it was not. How could it be? How could it affect my life in *any* way? I had never seen it before in my life.

I tried to shake myself out of the melancholy. I actually physically shook my head and my shoulders. Why would my parents have buried anything in the backyard? That just wasn't like them. The only reason Amelia Star would ever lay shovel to earth was to plant flowers. And Dad? He never picked up a shovel, not even to remove the winter snow. The grounds were too large and there were too many pathways and too much driveway. I was thinking of the circular, interlocking stonework out front. He had people for that. Well-paid people. And they came on a regular schedule.

I arrived at the conclusion that this urn did not belong to my folks. It must have been buried ages ago by some previous owner.

My parents had lived in this house for over thirty-five years. The house itself was much older than that. But it had undergone several remodels resulting in the beautiful refurbished, architectural mix of old and new that it was today.

I was tempted to unwrap the plastic from the urn to see what it really was. But at the moment I had no time. I left the urn on the coffee table and exited the atrium. As I passed through the kitchen, a glance at the digital clock on the stainless-steel microwave informed me that the day waned. I wanted to talk to Charlie about the little black and tan Cavalier. All my calls to the center today had gone to voice mail. He was away from the desk. The week before Christmas was a busy time, and I should probably just stop by and talk to him.

I drove straight to the gardening center that was just outside of town. A large placard in bright green and black read:

ROSE & LILY Garden Centre

It was a fine-looking sunshiny afternoon. When I arrived Charlie was nowhere in sight, but Lily who was hooked to her leash was curled up in a brown donut bed filled with doggy toys beside the payment counter. "Hi cuddle-buns," I said extending a hand to her probing snout. "What are you doing here? Where's Daddy?"

On occasion Charlie would take Lily to work with him, but mostly he left her at home. She was perfectly fine alone and well behaved. He never came home to streams of toilet paper all over the bathroom or chewed up slippers and shoes.

The only time he took her to work was when repairmen were at the house. As far as I knew nothing was broken.

Lily climbed out of her bed and tried to snuggle into my lap as I squatted in front of her, rubbing her ruffled rump and making me laugh. A voice abruptly interrupted our play, asking, "Hey, what are you doing here? I thought you had an eye appointment?"

My head jerked sideways. My nerves were in

that kind of state where you jumped at every unexpected sound.

Turned out I wasn't the only one that was jumpy. Charlie was acting strange. And it was Charlie who had snuck up behind me—with the largest poinsettia plant I had ever seen—in his arms. His voice sounded a bit on edge, which was very unlike him. It didn't usually bother him if I popped by his work for a visit. As a matter of fact, if I recalled correctly, he had been pleased.

I answered hesitantly as I dragged myself to my feet, one hand on the top of the cashier's desk for support. I said, quite lightly, "I went to the eye appointment and I'm fine."

Lily danced over to Charlie.

"No, Lily," he remonstrated. "I can't pet you right now. I don't want to drop this oversized posy on you." He was trying to cover up his brusqueness, but it wasn't working. He must have realized that his question sounded like an accusation, like my sudden appearance was not only a surprise, but unwelcome.

I lifted the sunglasses to show him my eyes. To diffuse the tense situation, I attempted a false light-heartedness even though I had no idea what was causing it. "See? Whatever those eye drops were that Toby gave me they're already working. It's probably the same stuff that Leo prescribed for Lily." A hearty chuckle escaped my lips unchecked. "The scary pinkeye is almost gone." I shoved the sunglasses over my hair to show I no longer felt self-conscious.

Best to keep the conversation rolling to ease the awkwardness. My finger stabbed in the direction of the gargantuan poinsettia that was beginning to sag in his grip. The velvet crimson foliage had a span of at least four feet, and the height of the plant was nearly the same. Good thing Charlie was tall. "What are you going to do with that?" I asked.

Apparently, his mind was elsewhere and he did not hear me. In the silence that followed I couldn't help but notice just how tall he was. I had always had a thing for height. Even with the plant causing him to stoop a little he remained a solid six feet. He was wearing a thick, dark moss green wool sweater with sleeves pushed up to the elbows. The tendons of his neck were taut and I could see the tension there. His gaze was not focused on me but on the ground like he was deciding where to put the plant.

"Can I help you with that?" I casually tapped one of the leaves of the poinsettia.

He shook his head, sent a furtive glance backwards at the door. What did he not want me to see? I made a tentative peek around the poinsettia by straining my eyes, before drawing them swiftly back as his forearms flexed and he shifted the pot in an attempt to retrieve my attention.

"What's the matter?" I asked. "What's going on out there?"

"Nothing, Sophie." He had spoken my name a

little loudly and it startled Lily into getting excited. Were we going for a walk? That was always a canine's first thought.

"Not yet, Lily," I said to her. She was clawing my knees and wagging her tail energetically, slapping several potted flowers that were on the floor and knocking one over. Dirt went flying along with the pills of Styrofoam used for soil drainage. The more I tried to quiet her excitement the more excited she became. Ordinarily an antic like this would have made me laugh, but clearly neither Charlie nor I were in a laughing mood.

Finally, I lured Lily off to the side, picked up the toppled pot and placed it heavily onto the cashier's desk.

Charlie sat the large poinsettia down on the floor. I swear he had positioned it deliberately to block my view of the doorway. Now he returned his gaze to me. "I'm donating this to the church," he chattered inanely. He was copying my offhand mood. "Along with all of those red and white Christmas flowers on the floor there that were delivered to me by mistake. Including that one our girl just knocked over. By the time the supplier is able to come back for them they'll no longer be fresh and saleable, so after an hour or so of negotiating last night, I agreed to keep them."

"But that means you'll have to take a loss," I said. "Are they going to substitute with the poinsettias?"

"Oh, they'll deliver them by tomorrow, but the return truck is not the same as the delivery truck. So, I'm kind of stuck with them—and the bill. But it's for a good cause."

"You're so kind, Charlie. You'll also go broke if you keep being so generous."

He grinned. "As long as I have you and this little monkey, and this gardening center I'll always be rich." The little monkey, aka Lily, tied to crawl up his leg.

It seemed that whatever was bothering him when he first discovered me here with her had vanished. I reached up and kissed him on the lips. "You are so schmaltzy."

"Thank you, sweetheart. You flatter me." He kissed me back.

I dropped my arms. "Hey, I have a favor to ask. Is this a bad time?"

He hedged for an instant. "No. Shoot."

What I was about to ask was going to sound strange to him because it sounded strange to my own ears. But I never got the chance to ask because his phone suddenly chimed. In a way I was relieved because I hadn't yet figured out how I was going to explain my sudden request.

"It's okay go ahead, what did you want to ask me," he said, glancing briefly at the caller ID. "They can call me back."

"No. You answer it. I *did* come at a bad time. You're at work and it could be business." In fact, it was almost definitely business.

"Are you sure?"

I nodded.

He shrugged and did as I suggested. He avoided mentioning the person's name as he took the call, and turned aside to face the door and the two windows. His body language was uncharacteristic. He was typically so relaxed, and open. Normally, he had nothing to hide. He listened a while, and then disconnected the call. For an unnerving second, I wondered if it wasn't my mother.

"It's a customer, honey. I need to deal with it straight away." He gave me a searching look. "Can this favor wait until tonight when I get home? I'll call you at your parents' place."

"Yes, yes, of course. You're busy. I can see that. But you don't have to do that. I can come over."

Several thoughts were spinning in his head all at once. Whatever they were he gave no indication to me. I only knew—no—felt that he was trying to divert me from going to his house. When I raised my eyebrows in query his answer surprised me. "No."

No?

He must have realized how abrupt that sounded because he immediately corrected himself by saying: "I mean. Why don't we meet for dinner? I've missed you. I want to take you out."

But I had other ideas. Namely, why didn't he want me to come over? What was the big deal?

I was beginning to feel like a wet rag, thoroughly indecisive. And yet it wouldn't do to seem suspicious, until I knew for certain there was something to be suspicious about.

"Sophie?" Charlie said. "What about it? Let's go out for dinner."

I shook the disturbing thoughts out of my head. "Sure," I answered.

His lips formed a thin line, not quite smiling. There was clearly something occupying his thoughts. He dusted off his pants and looked at me. "Wait here. I'll be back in a few minutes."

He seemed nervous again. Who had called? What was going on? I was incapable of shutting off the repetitious feedback loop.

He abandoned the giant poinsettia on the floor where he had set it, blocking my view. Its canopy of rich crimson fanned at eye level like a patio umbrella. The flash of a smile meant to reassure me did nothing but fuel my curiosity more as he skirted around it to the door. I felt anything but reassured.

"Stay here, Lily," I said and made sure her leash was still attached to the hook on the wall. The lime green nylon strap coiled into a nest behind her bed. I crept back from behind the cashier's desk and hauled myself to my feet. I glanced down at Lily and whispered, "I'm going to see what Daddy is up to."

I slipped outside into the bright sunshine and stepped into the shadow of the building. I walked through the Christmas tree section to the chain link fence. In the parking lot Charlie's back was to me. He was speaking to a woman next to a blue Honda SUV that was parked beside my Lexus. She was a stranger to me. She was decked out in a confection of stylish, dark chocolate wool coat with fur cuffs and collar. She wore her copper-gold hair in a short ponytail. Her full mouth was accentuated with a bronze frosted lipstick. I would say she was attractive—pretty even—and dressed very unsuitably for purchasing a Christmas tree. Who was she? And why did Charlie not want me to see her?

I ducked back behind the shadows of the trees when his head turned slightly. Fortunately, he never saw me. I parted the boughs of a balsam fir, and peeked out.

The woman handed Charlie some papers and he studied them. A few moments later he returned them to her. She looked up into his face and smiled.

Either she was flirting with him or he had just told her something she wanted to hear.

I wished that I could get closer so that I could discern just exactly what they were discussing. Or see what those papers were. But the fence was in the way, and even if it wasn't there was no other obstruction to hide me. I should just walk around the fence to the gates and introduce myself. But how was I going to explain why I wanted to? It was clearly none of my business. And Charlie would have introduced me if he wanted me to know her. Who was she? I felt like slapping myself about, to return me to my senses. I was being obsessive.

My heart was doing rapid-fire flips. I was getting all bent out of shape. His meeting with her was probably innocent. If I had had my wits about me I would have known that. But what little wits I had left after that stupid cracked diamond dream, the great hot pepper fiasco and reuniting with three of my exes in three days, I could well be described as witless.

A terrifying idea occurred to me. Was she why he wanted me to go to stay with my parents?

No. Charlie wasn't like that. If he wanted to call off the engagement, he would just do it up front.

I was hyperventilating now. The two of them standing together made a handsome couple. The contrast of his rugged good looks to her stylish prettiness made for a picture perfect moment. This was absurd. My imagination was running away with me. I had to confront him. Now!

I know what I can do. I can ask him if he wants me to take Lily home, I thought. That would give me an excuse to interrupt them.

As I was churning all of this over in my mind, I suddenly realized that Charlie was gone. The woman was inside her car and preparing to pull out of the parking space. I hurried between the piquant firs, pines and spruces and wove my way back, but before I reached the doorway Charlie materialized in my path.

"Where'd you go?" he asked. He was slightly breathless as was I. Was his heart pounding as hard as mine? I thought for a moment that if the stupid thing hammered any harder, he would hear it.

I made a concerted effort not to squirm. Ironically so did he. "I—I thought I would look for a Christmas tree for my parents," I mumbled. *Whew. Good save.*

He frowned. "You were in the tree lot?" His gaze darted nervously over the chain link fence before returning to my face. "Your folks bought one from me a week ago."

Think fast. Or just tell the truth. "Oh. I thought it would be nice to have one inside the new atrium."

"Oh? Okay... Did you find one?"

"No. I probably should ask my mom first if she wants one in the atrium."

Lame. This guessing game had to stop. It seemed Charlie agreed with me because he abruptly asked, "Sophie, are you okay?"

No. I was not. But I wasn't about to let him know it. "Yes-yes. I'm great. So where did you want to go for dinner?"

"How about Quatrefoil?"

My heart stopped. Quatrefoil was a fancy place. A restaurant where you went to propose (as I well knew) or to break up. He had already proposed to me so he wasn't planning to do that. I sucked in a breath. My heart felt like it was doing acrobatic contortions. Why was I unable to confront him with my concerns?

Because they were ridiculous that's why. I exhaled. "Great. I'll meet you there. What time?"

"Seven thirty?"

"Yes. Seven thirty. Sounds good." I nodded my agreement.

He kissed me on the lips and I waved goodbye to Lily through the doorway. If I hurried maybe I could catch up to Miss Blue Honda SUV. Oh yes, you misjudged me. I had not forgotten about her.

I dived into my car. As Charlie turned to go inside, I backed out of my parking spot and made a left onto the road. There was almost no traffic. I would risk a speeding ticket if I hurried, but hurry I must.

I had witnessed her turn left. This road only went in one direction. I followed it and, lo and behold, a few minutes later I caught up with the blue SUV at a stoplight. She sat while the light seemed to stay interminably red. She dragged down the visor to fuss with her hair in the mirror. I hadn't been mistaken; she was disturbingly good-looking.

Her eyes remained focused forward on the road so she did not sight me. Even had she glanced in her rearview mirror all she would have seen was a stranger in a satin gray Lexus. Why would she care? She was clearly ignorant of any connection I had to Charlie, so why would she recognize my car?

I followed her for about a mile and then she

made the turn I was hoping she wouldn't.

She drove right up to Charlie's house and parked in the driveway.

CHAPTER 12

What was she doing at Charlie's house? How long had this been going on? She must have been furious when she discovered that I was coming to stay with him for Christmas. NO. No—no—no. It was all a mistake. This could not be happening.

I watched her ponytailed, lithe form—in those damnably fashionable fur cuffs and collar—skip up the stairs and unlock the front door. She went inside as easily as pudding slid down the throat. She knew her way around his house. That was obvious. A person who was entering someone's house for the first time would be hesitant, tentative as they figured out the nuances of an unfamiliar lock and key. Why did she have a key?

She had strolled into his house like she belonged there. It was impossible for me to stay after witnessing that.

I remained outside the driveway, idling parallel

to it. She had not seen me. I must go home. I must leave before she looked out the window or something, and spotted me. I had to figure this out.

I stepped on the gas and shot past the house. I was hot and bothered and confused despite the December weather. What was I going to tell Mom?

The road stretched ahead. Steam rose from the melting snow. The sky took on a golden red hue and the clouds curded in floating masses, gray and yellow-edged like healing bruises. I took the long way home. I needed the time to calm my nerves and compose myself. Why was I even so upset? There could be any number of reasons why a strange woman would have the key to his house—and why he hadn't informed me that she did. One thing was certain; she was not the house cleaning service.

It was dark by the time I rolled down my parents' street.

I left the car parked out front in the circular driveway. The key clicked in the front door. The alarm system was already disarmed. Inside the house the noise of the big screen TV blasted from the living room. The size of the screen matched the loudness of the audio. Dad's hearing was not what it once was, and I wasn't about to play the baddie and inform him of the fact. But it meant that my parents were home. I popped my head in the doorway to say hi to my dad. He was busy reading the paper but looked up for me to plant a kiss on his cheek.

"Did you have a fun day?" he asked.

Dad didn't notice my distraction. I was good at hiding my feelings. But I wanted to talk to Mom. I did not tell him about my eyes or the escapade with the Scorpion peppers. I did mention the fact that I was impressed with their new atrium. And that reminded me...

"Mom's in the sunroom," he said, not noticing my eyes at all. I glanced in the foyer mirror on my way through. My eyes had all cleared up. Whatever those drops were that Toby had given me had worked like a charm.

I passed through the kitchen noticing that my mother had found her phone, as it no longer sat by the stove. I followed the sounds of tumbling water until I neared the region of the fountain. Recessed lighting between multiple skylights illuminated the twenty-foot-high glass room. My parent's continued to call it a sunroom, but its grand scale really deserved a better term, which was why I called it the atrium.

Amelia was sitting at the cast iron sofa on the turquoise and orange cushions, her back against a pillow, facing the fountain, a gardening magazine splayed open on her lap. With the gurgling sounds of the fountain, she didn't hear me. She was talking on the phone and I didn't want to interrupt her so I stayed out of her line of vision.

"I'll try," she was saying. I had no idea who she was talking to. "But it will be hard to keep her away, she's so strong-willed."

Who was she talking about? Me? And if so, what did she want to keep me away from?

"You're a dear," she said. "One in a million. Talk to you later." She disconnected the call and I stepped out from the shade of a palm tree. I raised a hand in salutation.

"Who were you talking to?" I asked.

She jerked her eyes in my direction, startled, and laughed it off. "Oh, just the contractor."

I raised my brow and she gesticulated rather over-emphatically for me to join her on the couch.

I greeted her with a hug as I sidled in beside her. She had a cup of coffee on the table, half drunk, and set the phone down beside it.

"Did you pay the contractor, Sophie?" she asked, squeezing my hand.

"Yes." I went silent for a moment. "You were just talking to him. Didn't he tell you?"

She seemed flustered but what did I care what they had been talking about or even the fact that they had probably been discussing me. She had given me the opening I needed. There were so many questions I wished to ask her, so many answers I needed to hear. Why any of it mattered I don't know. I only knew that it had something to do with my past.

I withdrew my hand from hers and said, "He's not just the *contractor*, Mom. He's Abe Winslow. *My* Abe Winslow. Why didn't you tell me?"

My mom watched my expression for any overreaction. She pushed the gardening magazine off her lap and onto the coffee table. It was still splayed open to a page and now she closed it with a slap. I caught a glimpse of orange honeysuckle climbing up a tall white trellis from a thick bed of purple-blue periwinkle. Must be the spring issue because there was no plant life in winter worth doting on outside. She shoved the magazine with a manicured fingertip until it touched the glass bowl of green apples.

Her eyes tipped up. "I *did* tell you that I hired Abe Winslow. You were too preoccupied to hear."

"But I would have remembered if you had told me."

"It was almost a year ago when I signed the contract. You were just engaged to Charlie. You weren't paying attention. You had eyes and ears only for Charlie."

The mention of Charlie's name made me freeze. How could I talk about Charlie right now? The realization was too fresh, and I still had to discuss Rosie with him. More importantly, I had to find out what was going on with him before I jumped to any conclusions or made any future plans.

Mom leaned forward and picked up her vintage china coffee cup, "Do you want some, honey? There's a fresh pot in the kitchen."

At my nod, she got up and left to get me a cup.

It was then I noticed. The plastic wrapped silver

urn was gone. There was only the glass apple bowl, the magazine and her coffee cup with her phone beside it. No urn. Where had she put it?

I don't know why it popped into my head at this moment, but I was suddenly curious about our family pet.

I walked over to the threshold between the kitchen and the atrium. Amelia was busy pouring me a cup of coffee so I called across the long kitchen island. "Mom, how long did we have Jo Jo?"

She hesitated, mid pour, the metallic coffee urn raised in her hand. She preferred the old-fashioned coffee machines rather than the ones that used pods. Her face turned towards me. "Why this sudden interest in the dog?"

"I—I just can't remember him. And it kind of bugs me."

Her fingers were squeezing the handle of the coffee cup, her knuckles turning white. "Well, it was so long ago. He was a nice dog, like all dogs. We didn't have him for very long."

I paused. "Your allergies were *that* bad?"

She was clearly getting agitated. I was beginning to feel guilty for pressing her on the topic. Did *she* feel guilty about giving away my dog because of her allergies?

It wasn't important. How could it be important? It wasn't worth making her feel bad.

I swung back to the atrium and my eyes landed once more on the coffee table where the urn had been. I was feeling tightly wound and a little melodramatic. I should probably go and take a nap before my evening with Charlie. I wanted to be rested when I confronted him.

But my brain wasn't ready to let it go. What would happen if I mentioned the urn to Mom? The tension between us was palpable. Why? It was only something Abe's workman had dug up out of the soil. I'll bet there were dozens of vases and urns that were dug up out of peoples' gardens every year. In fact, I had witnessed a few unearthed myself during site visits in my landscape design jobs. They usually were broken things that someone had discarded. They were put into the dumpster and taken to the landfill.

"Are you okay, Sophie? You seem distracted," Mom said coming towards me, cup in hand.

I answered, "Oh, it's nothing. I'm just tired. I saw Toby today. He says my eyes are fine. He gave me some drops."

"So glad to hear it. They *do* look better. In fact, they look completely normal. What a talented doctor he is." She handed me the coffee cup and smiled. "How *is* our Dr. Jerome anyway?"

I proceeded to relate to her the sum total of my knowledge concerning my number two ex. She was surprised to learn that he was moving, and so far away. I then excused myself to get dressed for my date with my fiancé whom I desperately hoped was not about to be ex number four.

CHAPTER 13

Quatrefoil is a lovely restaurant inside a restored old home. It sits on the corner of Sydenham Street on a fenced in lawn that is green and lush in the spring and filled with color. Right now, snow covered the grounds and icicles dangled from the overhanging trees that gazed down on the stone patio. As I turned the corner from the angled parking lot after locking my car remotely, a glow of yellow light caught my eye. Between the cast iron spindles of the front gates that opened onto the patio, I saw three or four fire lamps lit up alongside eight outdoor tables. It was too cold for me to sit outside and I went in.

I thought I would feel awkward coming to this restaurant, especially since I had just seen Abe. The ambience was as I remembered it when he brought me here. But it wasn't Abe Winslow that was on my mind tonight. The rust-brown tile floors, glowing white walls and gumwood trim around the ceiling gave the space an elegant yet intimate feel. Overhead, a silver chandelier with glass candles gave off a quiet light. And on the walls, in muted tones, was modern art. The waiter sat me at a perfect corner table in a dark leather nook.

Charlie was late. Was his mistress keeping him? I thought, viciously.

Why was I doing this to myself? I sipped on my aperitif, a glass of white wine, trying not to spill it on the crisp white tablecloth, and twisted the diamond on my finger. I had no real evidence that he was playing around. I was just feeling stupidly insecure. Was it a mistake to agree to marry him? Did he think so, too?

I sighed, glanced at my phone. He could at least call or text. Why should I be the one to do it? Fifteen minutes more was all I would give him. The waiter came by and refilled my glass. The minutes passed. I finished the wine and glowered. This wasn't like him. He had better have a good excuse.

I was about to get up and leave in a huff when the waiter led Charlie to my table. He was dressed divinely in dress slacks, a pressed white shirt and light wool blazer. He had shaved, leaving a fashionable layer of stubble. He leaned over and kissed me on the cheek. "I'm sorry, sweetheart. I got held up."

I'll bet.

"Everything okay?" I asked innocently. Yeah-yeah, I was a hypocrite. Think one thing and say another. How did one even bring something like this up in casual conversation? It wasn't like he didn't have oodles of female customers. Because of course he did. It's just that they didn't usually have a key to his house.

What was I supposed to say: *'I followed that attractive customer of yours and she just happened to drive up to your house and open the door with a key and went inside?'*

Uh, then what?

Charlie was oblivious to my mental ramblings. He was busy explaining his tardiness. "Had to drive that shipment of flowers to the church and help them unload. Then the pastor needed me to help string up some Christmas lights." He tapped himself on the crown of his head, mischief in his eyes. "One of the disadvantages of being tall. People think you're a ladder with arms and fingers."

A flood of relief travelled swiftly through my system like an unchecked river. O-kay. And she had something to do with that. Maybe?

She was from the church. Sure, why not? It still didn't explain why he hadn't introduced me to her. But perhaps he had his reasons.

One of us was in a good mood and I was eager to join him. He seemed oblivious to my distraction and continued talking: "Turns out the Christmas tree I gave the church fit the space. At first, they thought it was going to be too big. I was ready with my saw however. Every problem has a solution." He grinned, leaned back well pleased with himself, and said, "Everything is on track."

What did that mean? I was missing something. What track were we talking about? That's what I got for allowing myself to get sideswiped.

I was about to ask him to elaborate when the waiter arrived. Charlie ordered a bottle of red wine and we perused the menus. The wine I had consumed before his arrival was beginning to affect me. I hoped I had not done or said anything unusual. I glanced at him hesitantly. "Is there some special reason you wanted to eat here?" I asked. "You hate fancy food."

His eyes danced with amusement. "I don't hate it. I just like comfort food better."

"Well, that's not what you're going to get here." I propped my elbows on the table and let my hands slide down my arms to the tabletop.

He reached across the table linen and cupped my left hand. His index finger touched the brilliant diamond in a tiny circular motion. "That's perfectly fine. We're here because *you* like it."

While his cheerful mood was a relief, much preferable to him suffering a guilt trip for being late, I have to confess I was confused.

The waiter returned with the wine, interrupting our conversation, and we gave our attention to the label. Surprisingly, Charlie knew a lot about wines. He and the waiter traded snippets about the nose and palette and various vintages of the label, and then Charlie sniffed the cork and swirled his glass prior to tasting before he nodded for the waiter to fill our glasses.

I was beginning to feel calmer now with the alcohol in my system and studied my fiancé's face. I decided to go with my first reaction. Whatever had happened today was something he was no longer disturbed by. He was definitely more relaxed than he had been this afternoon. He seemed very, very pleased with himself indeed.

"So, the problem with your customer all cleared up?" I asked.

"Oh that? Yeah. Everything has worked out great."

The image of the copper-gold ponytail and fur cuffs crossed my mind. I was nearly certain that *she* was that customer. I tapped my fingers on the menu to draw his attention. "Do I get to hear about it?"

"Eventually," he replied.

Eventually? His eyes oozed amusement and the corners of his mouth quivered. I frowned at him. He was laughing at me. Why, what had I done? The better question was what had *he* done?

The waiter came to take our order. I decided I was going to go all out tonight. I ordered the braised garlic duck leg with cranberry-mint-pomegranate salsa and roasted Brussels sprouts, and rosemary infused potato pancakes. He ordered filet mignon in a pepper brandy cream sauce with turnip and carrot mash.

"Cheers," Charlie said, raising his glass of burgundy wine. "To us."

I lifted my glass hesitantly. So, he hadn't brought me here to break off the engagement. I sipped my wine pensively.

Ever intuitive, Charlie frowned. "What's on your mind, Sophie? Are your eyes bothering you? He leaned in to get a closer look and I blinked at him.

"Are they still red?" I asked, knowing they weren't.

He shook his head. "In this light they look quite normal." He smiled. "In fact, you look strikingly beautiful."

That was exactly what a fiancé was supposed to say. Whether it was true or not was irrelevant. Nonetheless the compliment was appreciated. I crossed my legs fully aware of the black stilettos on my feet. Why was it that high-heels made a woman feel attractive? If it wasn't for that, I don't think any of us would wear them. They were a pain to walk in. Literally.

But no argument. They completed the outfit. I had made a last-ditch effort to dress for the occasion even though I had no idea what the occasion was. I wore an elegant green dress, fitted to the body with a low cut back. It stopped just above the knees and was sleeveless. The neckline fell in soft loose folds, a perfect accent to my emerald pendant.

I couldn't help but smile. The way Charlie was looking at me convinced me that Charlie didn't have a duplicitous bone in his body. So—this woman who had the key to his house must be no threat. Maybe she was a long lost relative. A cousin maybe?

Confession time. I was going to speculate on and off—until I knew the truth.

I wished I could stop being so distracted. Would it help if I told him about the dream?

"Sophie? What's on your mind?"

Maybe it wouldn't hurt if I told him part of it. I paused to mull things over, and then said bravely, "A couple of nights ago I dreamed that the diamond in my ring cracked in half."

The statement was blunt and it just slipped out. Good. If we were going to live happily ever after we had to trust each other. I needed to know what he thought of my dream. Was it premonition or anxiety?

Alas. I should have known better than to ask for his opinion. Just like a man. For him it was neither premonition nor anxiety about our upcoming marriage. But I was too tipsy to correct him. He captured my hand and studied the diamond. He rubbed it with his fingertip. "Tell you what," he said. "I'm going to take it in to my jeweler buddy tomorrow to make sure it's free of flaws. He'll do it on the spot. He owes me."

"No. That's not necessary," I insisted.

"If it's got you concerned, I think it is."

"No, Charlie, really, the diamond is perfect. I'm not worried that it might have a hairline fracture. I was just wondering what you thought... Oh, I'm just overthinking things. That dream was probably nothing, just a dream, a dumb old dream. You know how dreams are. They're often irrational and come out of nowhere, and make absolutely no sense. I'm fine. Please. Forget I mentioned it."

He did not. I got good and drunk, too drunk to drive myself home. And by the end of the evening, after we had made our way to his car, I surrendered the ring to him. He just happened to still have the little blue velvet box that it had come in when he proposed to me at the botanical garden last winter. It was in the glove compartment where it had lain for almost a year.

He slipped the precious piece of jewelry inside it, then into his inside jacket pocket, and promised to return it to me by Christmas day.

It was time to go home and I wanted to return to *his* place.

He smiled mischievously at me and took me back to my parents' mansion.

CHAPTER 14

I felt naked without the diamond. In the morning when my head was somewhat clearer, I phoned Charlie to request the return of my engagement ring. But the call went directly to voice mail. I had promised to meet Toby at the gardening center at noon. And I had forgotten to tell Charlie to bring Lily to work. I glanced at the time on my phone. Was he still home and just not answering? If not, the best solution was to just head over and fetch her. I still had the key. After all, when—if—we got married it would be my house too. And if he was there, I could ask him for my ring. He had misunderstood my whole purpose when I confessed about the dream. Why was I surprised? I was barely articulate last night.

"Mom," I said after breakfast. I felt like clutching at my throbbing head but forced myself to refrain. I was in no mood for a lecture on overindulging. Nor did I wish her to inquire as to the whereabouts of my engagement ring. I forced my left hand into my pocket, while gesturing with the right. "I'm heading over to Charlie's to get Lily."

"Lily?" My mom leaped from her barstool at the quartz kitchen island where she was sipping her second cup of morning coffee. "Oh, I'm sure Charlie has taken her to work with him. I—I mean, now that you're not there. He probably doesn't want to leave her alone."

She was acting kind of hedgy. Why didn't she want me to go over to Charlie's?

My phoned dinged and I glanced down at the text to see who it was. It was Toby confirming our meet and greet with the dogs at the gardening center. I felt frazzled. Had I drunk too much wine last night? From this stampede of elephants pounding in my head I would say: oh, most definitely. And then I realized I had left my car at the restaurant.

Oh great. That was just great. I had meant to confront Charlie about the strange woman with the key to his house but then I'd had the bright idea of telling him about the dream. Both attempts had failed. And where was my car? Still in the parking lot at Quatrefoil.

My phone dinged a second time to remind me of the text. And now here was Toby expecting me to bring Lily to meet Rosie. I knew my mom was watching me; her brows were furrowed in concern. Yes, I was acting weird. And maybe she was right.

What was I thinking? I had too much on the go to consider adopting a dog. And besides—I wasn't even sure I could do it. My thoughts were so messed up.

"Everything okay, honey?" she asked.

"Fine," I said. "I've gotta go. See you later." I waved a hand and realized my left hand had left my pocket and was displaying its nakedness.

"Sophie. Why aren't you wearing your ring?"

I went out the front door as though I hadn't heard her. I was going to fetch my car. I called for an Uber and as I waited in the drive, I saw Mom's face appear in the front window. The last thing I noticed her doing as the Uber pulled up in the circular driveway was put her phone to her ear. Who was she calling: a psychiatrist, perhaps? If any of my exes had specialized in psychiatry, you bet your life she'd be calling him.

No doubt, I needed to talk to someone. I wasn't ready to drag my parents into this. I had no real evidence that Charlie was doing anything wrong. And now I worried that maybe he had no intention of returning my engagement ring. *Am I stressed out or what?*

Meanwhile I needed to see Leo. I had no close friends left in Dundas. No gal pals. Only Leo— if you could call him a close friend. Leo would understand. Leo would talk me out of my craziness.

Would he think it strange? Why was it that, a decade after our breakup, it was Leo I felt I could talk to?

It just happened that he was free. His shift at the animal hospital didn't start until one this afternoon. Around the time I was supposed to meet Toby. Good. That would give us a couple of hours to chat.

I ended my conversation with Leo as the Uber arrived in the parking lot of Quatrefoil. I changed vehicles after paying the driver and drove the ten minutes to our rendezvous point. I shut down my phone before I exited the car. That should put a stop to any interruptions during our visit.

Leo met me in the parking lot at Webster's Falls as scheduled. He was already there sitting in his car when I pulled in. This time of year, there was practically nobody here. Other than our vehicles there were only two others. The air was still. Songbirds warbled. Chickadees flitted from one bare branch to another, sometimes landing on the exterior twigs and making the dead leaves still clinging there, quiver. The sky in the background was a sharp blue with wisps of cloud.

The crunch of our footsteps in the mix of snow and frosted leaf litter were the only ones we heard. I glanced back and then ahead of me. The wooded trail was empty except for a cardinal whose bright red plumage with black markings contrasted deeply with the snow. It fluttered into a low-hanging oak branch, black with frozen melt-water as we approached.

"Do you remember how we used to skip classes in high school and come here?" he asked. "We had such a blast, climbing down the gorge so that we could take pictures of the frozen waterfall from below.

There was a narrow metal staircase descending to the shallow pool where the swollen creek cascaded down in a sheet of rainbow water. The falls was frozen this time of year into ribbons of sparkling ice. Oh yes. Those were the days. Free of responsibility.

By this time, we had walked into the park area that in summer was a sumptuous green lawn but was now a blanket of untouched snow.

Memory became reality and I welcomed the view. Over the winter landscape a stone bridge crossed the wide, frozen stream that flowed over the gorge creating the stunning 22-meter-high cascade of falling ice. About 24 meters across, we could see to the other side where crystalized snow clung to the bare branches of dormant deciduous trees and thick, furry evergreens. "I always loved this place," I admitted.

His head bobbed enthusiastically. "Great place to take your dog."

"You have a dog?" I inquired. Oh, naturally he had a dog. He was a vet.

"Actually, I have two dogs and a cat."

I laughed. "Two dogs and a cat, two kids and another one on the way. That is *one* busy household," I remarked good-naturedly.

He smiled. He was not about to contradict me. He had a pretty perfect life. "So, what was it that you wanted to talk to me about?" he asked.

I felt my brow crease. I knew I was imposing, but if anyone would understand it was Leo. And even though we hadn't seen each other in a decade, seeing him again at the clinic and for dinner the other night had brought back all of those feelings of trust. There was a time when I could talk to Leo about anything. I hoped his wife didn't mind me stealing him from her like this. But it would only be for an hour or so.

He adjusted his tuque and glanced over at me. The wind gusted and his cheeks glowed from the cold. He said, "I know it must be important or you wouldn't have texted me."

I shrugged. "I'm not sure how important it is. It's just that you've known me a long time. Maybe you can understand what I don't."

"Okay. Try me."

We had crunched across the park's pristine snow, and now stood on the historic stone bridge admiring the vista. "Gorgeous, isn't it?" he said. "I love it when the waterfall freezes. It's like a stop-motion photograph. Ice crystals everywhere. Unfortunately, in order for it to look like this it has to be insufferably cold. Brrr." He mock shivered like a dog, drew his eyes away from the scenery and they landed firmly on me. "That isn't why you wanted to meet me though. What's up, Sophie? How can I help you?"

I paused to think. There were actually two things I wished to discuss with him. Number 1: the dream about the cracked diamond in my engagement ring. Number 2: The dog Rosie.

Where to begin? I hedged. I would start with the dream.

"I meant to ask your opinion on this the other day when we met for dinner at Betula." I was wearing mitts so Leo had no way of knowing that my ring finger was bare. I waited a moment to collect my thoughts. "Do you think dreams are premonitions?" I asked.

"No," he answered.

I arched a brow. "Never?"

"Never. Why?"

I sighed. "I had a dream a couple of nights back. In that dream, the diamond on my engagement ring cracked in half."

"Ah." His serious expression showed a glimmer of humor like he was trying to evaluate my reaction against his. "I wouldn't worry about that. It was just a dream. You're anxious and for good reason. Everyone is anxious when they decide to tie the knot."

"Were you?"

"Absolutely. Ask my wife. In fact, Sloane confessed that the night before our wedding she burst into tears and her mom thought she didn't want to marry me. But that wasn't it. She was just overwrought. So much to do in so short a time. She was fine on the day. Me? The night before I was putting milk in the cupboard and ice cream in the fridge. Yeah, it melted and made a mess. And the milk had to be thrown out."

"I told Charlie about the dream."

He glanced over. "What did he say?"

"He actually didn't speculate on what the dream meant at all. He thought I was worried that the diamond might have a hairline fracture and might at some point crack. He took the ring to the jewelers this morning. At least that's where I assume he went because I couldn't get hold of him when I called. I just want the ring back. I don't care if it's perfect. I just want our marriage to be. And now I'm worried that he doesn't intend to return it." I blushed because it was an embarrassing admission.

Leo guffawed at that. "Sophie, Sophie, Sophie. That's ridiculous. You really are in a tizzy, aren't you? Of course, he intends to return it. He's just doing what guys do. When a man loves a woman, he wants her to be happy. If your ring is flawed, he wants to fix that. Let him. And as for your marriage being perfect, whose is? Mine isn't. Sloane and I have a hectic schedule and a big family. We know we have to be aware of each other's moods and feelings. We love each other and it makes all the other stuff less hard. Marriages aren't perfect. But they work—if the people involved are well matched. If you meet the right person, you will weather all the ups and downs. I know. Sloane and I have been together now for eight years."

"Well—" I nudged him in the ribs with an elbow. "You *are* pretty perfect, and *I* should know. Lucky her."

He shook his head. "No. Lucky me."

"I guess I'm just over-reacting. It's been an astoundingly, over-stimulating three days. Did I tell you I also met up with two other of my exes since you?"

"Oh, geez. That *would* be stressful," he said, and laughed.

"I won't get into it, and I know you have to return to work. Are you still at the Spencer Creek hospital?"

"Yes and no. My upgrades are done. I'm moving back into my clinic. Have appointments right after the New Year. Meanwhile, this is my last day at Spencer Creek."

Speaking of which, this was my opportunity to bring up the second subject I needed his advice on.

"You know that poster of the little black and tan Cavalier that's taped to the wall at the Spencer Creek animal hospital?" I inquired.

"Oh, you mean Rosie?" He paused and then his eyes animated on guessing. "You mean you were considering adopting her? Why, that's wonderful, Sophie!" Leo's whole face lit up like sunlight breaking through cloud.

"Wait—wait. Slow down. I—I haven't decided. I just have to decide in the next hour because the owner wants to meet—" Curiously, I failed to explain that the owner was also the man I had dated after Leo.

"So, what's stopping you?" Leo asked. "She looks like a great dog. And she's even got personality. Did you see the photos with her in the little hats? So stylish. You two were made for each other."

I laughed weakly. "That's just it, Leo. I don't know if I should. I've been having second thoughts. With all that's happened I just feel like I can't cope."

"What do you mean 'with all that's happened'? The only thing that happened is that you had a bad dream and you made a mistake in trying to dry a few chili peppers in the microwave. Unfortunately, Lily happened to be in the house with you when that happened. You didn't mean to injure the dog."

"But that's just it, Leo. I *did* injure the dog—"

"Whoa. Hold on a minute. That was a bad choice of words on my part. You did not injure Lily. She wasn't hurt. There was no permanent damage. And any discomfort she experienced was fleeting."

"That doesn't change the fact that I don't know how to take care of a dog. Maybe that's why my parents never let me have one when I was a kid."

It occurred to me then, that that statement was all wrong. I *did* have a dog, but maybe that was the reason they took it away. Maybe it wasn't because Mom had allergies but because I had messed up somehow. Had I hurt the dog? Lost the dog? Failed to feed it and it starved to death? Wait a minute. I was six years old. None of that was possible.

And yet I had this nagging feeling that if I got a dog now, I might screw up.

"Look at how I messed up with Lily. Charlie leaves me with her for one afternoon and I pepper-spray her in the face." I clapped my mittened hands over my mouth, before quickly drawing them back for fear that I had smeared lip-gloss all over my face. A quick glance at my fur-trimmed black mitts informed me that all was well in that department—no pink smears.

"You should probably ask your parents about why they refused you a dog, instead of making stuff up. And I repeat. You did not mess up with Lily. I saw how you were with her at the clinic. You're a great fur mama."

We continued our walk over the curve of the bridge and down the other side. Here we had access to the frozen creek. The ice was thick, green and translucent between the gaps of fallen snow. I felt like being reckless. A strange, surreal compulsion urged me to walk out onto it.

You see what I mean? I had reckless thoughts. How could I own a dog when any minute I might put its life in danger because I hadn't foreseen the consequences of my actions?

Leo had to get back to the clinic. I had to meet Toby. But first I had to go to Charlie's house.

CHAPTER 15

Charlie's home reminded me of a gingerbread house. It was tall and narrow, and shaped like a classic house with a sharply peaked roof where the attic was, and the front door was in the middle with a curtained window on either side. He had strung up lights, the kind with the oversized bulbs, all across the eaves and around the windows and doorframe and even on the railing of the porch. And they reminded me of the jellybeans and gumdrops I saw on the gingerbread houses in the bakeries during the festive season. Just thinking about it gave me a warm fuzzy feeling.

When I pulled up just short of the house, I sat inside my vehicle staring. There was no room to park. Charlie's red truck was still in the driveway. What surprised me even more was the blue Honda SUV in front of it. If *she*—if that *woman's* car was in front of Charlie's truck that meant she had either arrived first or she had spent the night.

I cannot describe the emotions that were conflicting in my brain. What was going on? But one thing I knew for certain. I was not about to leave.

I did not want to catch them in the act, but if this was the only way I could know for certain, then so be it. If my perfect gingerbread house dream was broken then I had to know what pieces were left for me to pick up.

I was feeling strangely calm. Maybe that was what determination did. I was resolute this time. There was no turning back—except I *did* have to back up my car because there was no place for me to park in the driveway. It only fit two cars single file.

Slowly, I reversed my vehicle, and left it on the side of the street.

I had my own key. I could not believe that Charlie would allow this woman to have a key when I was in town. Yes, every innocent excuse I had imagined to explain this woman's presence had gone the way of the fax machine. I was back to my original doubts. And that made me furious, and he was going to know it. I mean, *was* she some sort of ex-wife, and were those papers she had shown him the other day divorce papers?

I fumbled in my handbag for the key to Charlie's house. Just as I was about to insert it into the lock, the door opened, and Charlie stepped out. He nearly collided with me. Lily was at his feet and wormed her way out the door to greet me with a slap of the paws and a wet, sloppy kiss. She was so preoccupied with my unexpected appearance that she didn't even realize she was loose.

"Hello precious," I said, squatting to tickle Lily's chin. Dogs were innocent victims when their pet parents suffered discord. I wasn't going to let her know what I thought of her daddy's antics. "I've missed you."

Charlie quickly drew the door behind him until the latch clicked. I barely caught a glimpse inside. I saw nothing, said nothing.

"Hi, honey," he said, artificially cheery. He twisted the leash he had in his hand nervously. "What are you doing here?"

That was beginning to be a favorite phrase of his. Didn't he want me to appear unexpectedly anymore? He used to love it when I showed up spontaneously. Because I rarely did. That was one more thing between us that was different. He was spontaneous and I wasn't. When had that changed? When I was with Leo, and then Toby, I was more adventurous. That could be chalked up to youth and high spirits. But that was irrelevant to the current situation. I reiterate *he* was spontaneous and I was not. And this new behavior was only helping to feed my suspicions.

I gave Lily one last scratch behind the ears and stood up. No more beating around the bush. I had given him his chance to confess last night when I had asked about his mysterious customer. He had refused to recognize the opening and explain.

Well, no more pussyfooting around. I jerked my neck toward the blue SUV. My finger jabbed accusingly at the Honda. "Whose car is that?"

"Oh. I'm—" I could imagine the numerous excuses he might give. It belonged to the chimney sweep, the furnace guy, the dishwasher repairman. The I.T. guy. He didn't need an information technology specialist. *He* was it. I had never known anyone who didn't fix computers for a living that knew so much.

"Don't tell me it's the I.T. guy because I won't believe you."

He laughed nervously and stooped to hook a finger under Lily's collar. "It's not. The dishwasher has been acting up."

"That car belongs to a plumber?" *Ha.* He expected me to buy that? It was spanking new and shiny. A Honda Acura SUV. What kind of plumber drove a car like that to fix toilets?

"Look, Sophie..."

Yes. I'm listening.

He was still beating around the bush. He had no more excuses and opted for the facts. "I was just leaving for work," he said.

"With Lily?"

"Yes. Why not?" He continued to worry the leash with one hand as he tried to hook her up. When he succeeded, he gestured. "Come on. I'll walk you to your car. Glad you were able to pick it up this morning without any trouble. I called you earlier to tell you I was coming to pick you up so that we could get it together, but your mom said you had already left." His glance shifted from side to side, obviously distracted but making an attempt to focus on what he was saying. "Where did you park?"

He made to move forward, expecting me to follow, and I stepped in his path. It was obvious where I had parked. My satin gray Lexus was visible at the side of the road.

I planted both hands on my hips. "If you leave, I am going inside the house."

"Don't do that, Sophie."

I was dissatisfied at his response. "Why not?"

His phone dinged. I stared at him. He pulled it out of his pocket.

Was it her? Was it Miss Blue Honda SUV? Clearly, he thought this text would be a good distraction. Think again, buster.

Throughout this whole interaction I was acting out of character. I cannot emphasize this strongly enough. I am not spontaneous. Every move I make is plotted out. I was no longer Leo's teen girlfriend who skipped classes to visit frozen waterfalls. *I am not impulsive.* The last time I was impulsive was when I plucked the diamond engagement ring that Abe had placed on my dessert and returned it to him—before I dashed out the door. And yet some impulse made me snatch the phone out of Charlie's hand.

The Caller ID read Amelia Star—my mother. The message said:

> ***Can't reach her, Charlie.***
> ***Unable to stall.***

What? What were my mom and Charlie conspiring about? Did my mother know about the other woman?

Tears filled my eyes. Did my mom love Toby so much that she didn't want me to marry Charlie? But Toby was already married. He had a son!

I handed the phone back. I must be losing my mind. Mom would never stoop that low. Would she? My throat was so constricted with emotion I could not speak.

"Sophie, it's not what you think."

I struggled to keep my thoughts sane. "What *do* I think?"

"Well, I'm not sure exactly. But it's making you angry."

"I am not angry," I said. I was distraught. And perhaps a little crazy.

I could not take much more of this. I was about to go to my car and just give up and let whatever happened happen, when another vehicle nosed into the driveway. There was no room for it. But I recognized the vehicle. It was the big black truck that was parked outside my parent's house yesterday.

The bright four-way flashers went on. A tall man in a black parka got out. I gasped. He left his truck where it was half in the driveway, half out on the road, and wandered up to join us.

It was Abe. What was he doing here?

The two men shook hands. Abe nodded at me. I glanced from Charlie to Abe and back again. Charlie's face broke into a grin. What was he grinning about? I felt like my head was about to explode.

Lily skipped up to Abe to be petted. Lily knew Abe? She usually didn't go up to strangers without being introduced first. So, they must have met before. He squatted to pacify Lily, and then rose to his full height, which was nearly equal to Charlie's. They knew each other.

I watched the two men exchange sheepish looks.

"Guess the cat's out of the bag?" Abe said ruefully.

"Guess so," Charlie agreed.

What cat? What bag?

Oh my god. It suddenly dawned on me. Abe was a contractor. Then who was that woman? My eyes turned sharply towards the house.

"I see Kate is here already," Abe said to Charlie.

Kate. My mind did a circular entrenchment into my memory. *Kate.* How did I know that name? Then it hit me like a lightning bolt and I felt as sheepish as a lamb.

"*Your* Kate?" I said to Abe, facing him sharply. *The interior designer, Kate?*

"Yep." Abe nodded. He turned to Charlie. "Guess, I'll leave it to you to explain. Sorry the surprise was spoiled. But that's our Sophie. She's like a female Sherlock Holmes. Nothing gets past her.... Text me when you want to move your truck so that I can move mine out of the way and then park it in the drive." He smiled and went inside the house. The door had been left unlocked.

I turned to stare at Charlie. He was still standing there with a contrite expression on his features. "I wanted it to be a surprise, Sophie. Guess I can text your mom back and tell her you know."

What did I know? I grabbed his arm. "You're jumping the gun. Am I to presume that you are renovating the bathroom shower and my mother knows?"

He cupped my face between his hands and kissed me full on the lips. "You are a little nutcase sometimes. Of course, I'm renovating the shower. And not *just* the shower, the entire bathroom."

And he had wanted it to be a surprise.

"The demolition has been completed and the tiles are installed. We're waiting on the shower glass this morning. Kate brought the fixtures today." He smiled a little sheepishly. "I asked Abe to do the work because he knows your taste and his fiancée is an interior designer. She drew up the floor plan. Do you want to go inside and see? Maybe you want some things changed." He shoved one hand into his inside jacket pocket and removed a folded sheet of paper.

It was the design for the bathroom remodel. The papers she had been showing him at the garden center when I had inconveniently appeared. There were some changes that she had wanted him to sign off on.

I laughed with relief feeling stupidly childish and utterly foolish. I grabbed him by the wrists and pushed his hands away that were holding the design. "No—no. Don't show me. I want it to be a surprise. I know it will be perfect."

"Are you sure, Sophie? Now that it's no longer a *real* surprise, you may as well have it exactly the way you want it."

The way he had gone ahead at such short notice to initiate the renovation was exactly the way I wanted it. How many men would have the perception and the desire to act on his partner's secret wishes without her having to nag him?

And the fact that he had chosen Abe Winslow and his fiancée Kate, a team that was very likely to come up with something that would match my tastes—that was the clincher.

No. This was perfect.

I wiped away my tears feeling like an absolute fool. Wow. Talk about stressed. Charlie was right. I needed a real vacation, and not *just* a vacation. Maybe I needed to change my life. Get some priorities straight.

Problem was, I still wasn't quite sure what those were.

CHAPTER 16

I was so overjoyed that Charlie wasn't having an affair that I forgot all about Toby and Rosie until I was halfway home and Charlie had gone to the gardening center with Lily. I squinted into the sun, made a U-y on the empty road and headed west. I parked outside the chain link fence and walked up the gravel parking lot to the gates. Charlie was nowhere in sight, but I knew where I would find Lily.

I was right. She was inside, sleeping in her donut bed next to the cashier's desk. It seemed dark inside after the brightness of the outdoors. However, after my eyes had adjusted, I knew just where to look and could make out Lily's curled up form, head now raised as I approached. The giant poinsettia had been pulled out from the wall creating a huge, scarlet umbrella over her head.

I checked to make sure none of the leaves had fallen, although I knew Lily would never touch the leaves if they did. But these were fresh plants and not a single leaf had detached from the main stalk.

All of the red and white Christmas flowers that had sat on the floor had gone to the church yesterday so Charlie must be preparing the truck for the massive poinsettia tree. I must have just missed him.

I was about to go outside to see if I could find him when out of the dim interior, he appeared right in front of me.

"Hey honey. Thought you'd gone home to your folks to help with the Christmas decorations?"

"I was on my way when I realized I hadn't asked you what I had wanted to ask you the other day."

"Oh? What was that?" He stopped from scooping a scatter of tipped empty flowerpots off the floor and deposited them on the counter and looked at me. Before I could continue speaking, movement caught my corner vision. I turned to look. The bright rectangle that was the entrance was partially blocked, darkening the room. I glanced at the doorway and at the shadowy human silhouette standing there. It was a man with a dog. After a moment to orient themselves, they came in.

"*That*," I said.

Charlie turned. The man and dog approached and stopped in front of us. The dog's eyes lit up and she wagged her tail. Behind me I felt Lily stir.

I waved a hand. "Toby. Hi! You are so prompt." I glanced at Charlie whose puzzlement was being held at bay. He smiled amiably as he always did in case this was a customer. My eyes flipped from one man to the other. "Toby, this is Charlie Payne my fiancé. And Charlie this is Toby Jerome, the ophtha—the eye doctor I saw yesterday."

Charlie visibly relaxed. "*The* Toby Jerome?" he said.

"Uh huh." I forced myself not to blush. I turned to my number two ex. "Charlie knows that we dated in college."

Toby was equally at ease. "Great," he said. "So, we're like old friends. Nice to meet you Payne."

"Likewise, Jerome."

Toby's humor and charm were contagious. Charlie shook his hand. A swishing tail caught his attention and he glanced down. "And who do we have here?" Charlie stooped and held out his knuckles to Rosie. Lily took this as a cue to investigate the stranger.

As I watched the meet and greet between my current boyfriend and my ex and my current boyfriend's dog and my ex's dog, something weird overcame me. It was like that morning when I had the dream. Adrenalin shot through my system causing my heart to flutter. My breath shortened. I saw a flash of an image in my mind. Something cracked. Something broken. Something destroyed. A scrap of memory that I had forgotten. It had something to do with the dog.

Why did the sight of Rosie create this response

in me?

"What's the matter, Sophie?" Charlie asked. He had noticed my total inertia.

Toby sent a troubled glance at me. "Are you feeling okay? Are you having another bout of vertigo? Or is it your eyes that's bothering you?"

He stepped forward and without touching me, peered into my eyes. I jerked my head away. This had nothing to do with the pepper accident—or with my eyes.

Charlie stared at us, his puzzlement deepening.

"I'm fine, I'm fine. Stop fussing. You're such an old lady—" Such was my attempt to keep things light. Both men knew me well enough to do as they were told.

Meanwhile, I fought to keep control. My breathing was shallow but even. This would pass. Like last time, it would pass. I focused on the task at hand.

The two dogs appeared to like each other. Their tails were wagging and they were sniffing. Their body language was relaxed. They reminded me of those old oil paintings of royalty with their hunting dogs, King Charles spaniels, seated regally next to their aristocratic owners.

I bent down to stroke Rosie. Again, a flash, like a memory. Black and tan. The image of a dog. One just like this one, only younger, very much younger. Lying on its side.

"So, what do you think, Sophie?"

I tugged gently at Rosie's ears. I remembered doing this but not with Rosie or with Lily. I ran my hand down her back to her long feathery tail. Toby must have brushed her recently. Her hair gleamed like black lacquer. "She's such a charmer," I said, struggling to keep my voice from quavering. But my thoughts were still all over the place.

Toby glanced at Charlie. Charlie returned his look, doubly confused. Of course, he was. I hadn't had the chance to explain to him that Rosie was in need of a new home.

But now, more than ever, I was sure I was the wrong person.

These feelings I was experiencing were unsettling. How could a dog I had never met create such feelings of uncertainty in me? And let me elaborate. I didn't mean that I was unsure about adopting her, although I was, but this wasn't causing the strange visceral sensations. It was a feeling of fear, the fear of loss and the devastation that followed.

"Toby, I can't do this right now. I—I'll get in touch with you later. I—I—I have to go."

Now it was Toby that looked confused. But not surprised. Charlie was simply bewildered. He still hadn't clued in.

"What's going on, Sophie?" Charlie asked.

"I'll explain later. I have to go somewhere."

Toby's eyes widened as I stepped past him and out the door. I ran to my car and got into the front seat. Was I having a panic attack? I could hardly breathe. Out of the edge of my vision I saw Charlie walk Toby and Rosie to his car. Rosie leaped into the backseat like a pro. Toby slid into the driver's seat and started the engine. He had to get back to his practice anyways. Eye doctors were always behind schedule and I hadn't helped any by delaying him.

I pressed the ignition. Charlie was running up to my car now, taking a trajectory that put him right in my path so that if I started to move the car at any speed, I would run him over.

He grabbed at the hood of my SUV and swung himself down the side of it to the driver's window. He tapped on the glass and I had no choice but to lower it. "What happened?" he demanded. "Where are you going?"

"I have to see my mom."

"Okay. Why? Why right at this moment?" He paused to catch his breath. I was breathing easier by now as well. Out of the corner of my eye I saw Toby's car pass by, his wave tentative, and turn onto the road. Charlie said, "Toby explained why he brought his dog down here. It was to see if she got along with Lily because you're interested in adopting her. Is this true?"

I nodded. I shut my eyes and then opened them. He was still there. "But I don't think I should."

He fell quiet. Then said, "Why not? She needs a home. We *have* a home."

"Charlie," I whispered. I don't know why I

was whispering except that I felt exhausted and strangely defeated. *Don't ask me what I meant by that. I don't know what I mean.* "I just can't."

"He says we only have a couple of days to decide. He doesn't want to leave her at a shelter or the SPCA."

Tears were beginning to stream down my cheeks.

He yanked at the car door. It was locked.

"Open the door," he ordered.

"No. I have to go."

"You can't drive like that."

I was crying sincerely now. "Oh, Charlie, what's wrong with me?"

He reached over the rim of the window and unlocked the door. "Get out and go to the passenger side. I'm going to get Lily and then I'll drive you to your mom's."

CHAPTER 17

The folks were home when we got to their mansion. I knew because I could see the flashing of the TV in the living room through the sheers as we parked in the drive. And if Dad was home, then so was Mom. The only thing Dad did on his own since his retirement was to go golfing. Obviously, he wasn't golfing. And Mom never watched TV during the daytime.

I led Charlie around the side path to the new stone walkways that wove through the garden and up to the terraced patio. I had a key to the atrium and shoved it in the lock. I opened the door and a rush of warm air blew forward to meet us. I had stopped crying now. Lily was wagging her tail, curious as to what adventure we were about to embark on. I kicked off my boots and Charlie mimicked me. We left our wet footwear on the drying mat and padded in stocking feet around the bubbling fountain.

Charlie whistled. "This atrium is stunning."

I had no time for compliments; besides the compliment wasn't for me. It was a tribute to my mother's taste, her designer's talent and her contractor's craftsmanship. I went to the coffee table but naturally it wasn't there. Mom had moved it. Where? I returned to the bookcase where Abe had originally retrieved it and looked up at the top shelf. Why would it be there? Mom didn't know that that was where Abe had initially stashed it. Nonetheless I asked Charlie to look. He did, and then reached up to see if there was anything further back out of his view. There was not.

Sounds came from the kitchen. Voices. Then my mom appeared in the doorway.

"Hi kids. What a nice surprise! Why didn't you come through the front door? It was just by chance I happened to be in the kitchen. I'm making cranberry-orange scones and tea. Do you want some?" Then her face fell when she saw the look on mine. She rushed over to grab me by the shoulders. "Sophie, what happened? Are you hurt? Is it your eyes? What's the matter?" I don't know what thoughts were cascading through her mind. Her eyes travelled up to Charlie's accusingly and she said the first thing she thought of. "Were you at the house? Did she hate the remodel?"

"No," I said, flinging her hands away. "I love the remodel. I haven't seen it yet but I know I will love it when I do. No, it's not that." I turned to face my mom fully. "Mom," I said. "Where did you put that urn that Abe left on the coffee table yesterday?"

I saw my mother exchange a look with Charlie. He shrugged. In the car, on the drive over, I had tried to explain what I had felt upon seeing the tiny silver cremation urn. Obviously, I had failed.

"I'm not sure I understand, Amelia," he said. He glanced from me to my mother. "Sophie says there was some kind of cremation urn that was dug up out of your garden during the renovation. Your contractor Abe Winslow showed it to her."

"Where is it?" I demanded, my hands flailing in the air. Why they were flailing of their own accord, I have no idea. My body seemed to be doing things that I was not in control of.

"I'm not sure what you're talking about, dear," my mom said. Whether the comment was meant for me or Charlie was unclear. She was looking at neither of us. Instead, her vision was focused on the glass wall beyond the fountain and the potted trees towards the outdoor terrace.

"The silver urn. It was wrapped in plastic. Abe showed it to me yesterday. He thought it might be something you wanted to keep." I scowled. I was getting really frustrated now. Why wasn't she cooperating with me? "Who is in it?"

"There is nobody in it," Mom whispered.

Dead silence greeted me. She was lying. There were only two reasons Amelia Star would lie. To protect me or to protect herself—if telling me the truth would jeopardize our relationship. But in the end, I knew that even if she was protecting herself, it was really in order to protect me. True, that explanation sounds confusing, and maybe even a little irrational. But that was my mother.

"Amelia," my dad's voice came from behind her. Charlie and I turned to look. Even Lily seemed interested in the newcomer. She had met my dad once or twice before and was thinking about hopping over to the kitchen to reacquaint herself. He had one hand on the side of the wide portal between kitchen and atrium. "I think it's time she knew."

"Knew what?" I demanded.

Another maddening silence descended as my dad sent a firm look at his wife.

"We should never have saved it," she said.

My father came into the atrium and put an arm around her. He squeezed her reassuringly. "Tell Sophie what is in that urn. I'll go and get it."

He waited for her response but she merely slumped right where she was standing. I swear if Dad hadn't still been supporting her slight weight she would have collapsed in that very spot. "Amelia," he said. "It's the right thing to do."

He left the room.

I glared at her. What big mystery had they been keeping from me? And why? My mom was having trouble dragging her eyes away from the direction Dad had gone. Below my knees, the *swish-*

swish of Lily's tail drew my attention. I was about to demand where Dad had gone, where had they hidden the urn and what was in it when I guessed before I even ventured to ask. I moved toward Mom and touched her hand that was clasped to her mouth. "Is it Jo Jo?"

She nodded and dropped her hands. Her eyes filled with tears. "You remember?"

I sank down on the sofa and started to cry. It was all coming back to me now. It happened on Christmas Day. It happened twenty-six years ago, but it might as well have been yesterday. Mom sat down beside me and wrapped her arms around me. "I didn't want you to remember, Sophie. It was so horrible for you. You were only six years old and Jo Jo was only three. I shouldn't have kept the urn. I should have let the vet take care of it."

It was a relief to let the emotion out. I had no idea how long I had held this memory in check. My thoughts were ragged, scrambled, little scraps of images, puppy dogs and little girls and pretty hats. My tears were starting to dissipate. No. *Let them come.* I wanted to remember.

I was thirty-two years old. It should not hurt so much.

Dad came in with the urn. He placed it in my hands and kissed the top of my head. The urn was unwrapped from its plastic casing. The metal was still remarkably untarnished. It held the cremated remains of my little puppy. My Jo Jo.

Charlie squatted at my knees. Lily tried to get up on them. He patted her down. Strangely it was comforting to have her there. "I'm so sorry, Sophie. I didn't know."

How could he know? The only two people who remembered the tragedy had kept it a secret for almost three decades. Was that the right thing to do? Would *I* have done that if it were *my* child? I remember thinking not too long ago that people had unusually strong attachments to their dogs. I almost thought they had *unnatural* attachments to their dogs. But I had never dared say that out loud for fear of offending people who loved their dogs.

My wet-lashed eyes turned up to seek Charlie's. Natural or unnatural made no difference. It was true. Dog love was a special kind of love, and you could feel it at any age. Lily reached up and licked a tear that clung to my chin.

I wasn't angry with my parents. I understood how difficult it must have been whenever the subject of a pet dog came up. They had done what they thought best. What they didn't know was how that incident would affect my relationship with everyone I would ever love.

I felt Charlie's hand come overtop my own. He twined his fingers with mine. It was a reminder of how strong attachments could be. Should be.

There was nothing unnatural about my attachment to Jo Jo.

It was true I remembered very little now. What

my parents had tried to do was erase that day from my memory. But things like that cannot be erased. They affect relationships.

"Oh, Sophie, I didn't know," Charlie repeated.

I managed to whisper, "I didn't know either."

But I had always known something. It was no wonder my parents had not wanted to buy me another dog. It was something no child should have to see. No person for that matter. It had happened right in front of me. I was holding the leash. My mother had had to grab me to keep me from rushing out onto the busy street. Jo Jo had slipped his collar and was hit by a car.

That was why the following Christmas we went to Florida.

They say that a dog can steal your heart. Everyone who has ever had the privilege to share his or her lives with a dog knows that this is true. You do everything to take care of it, to love it, to nurture it, and sometimes even then fate takes a cruel turn. I understand why my mom wanted me to forget.

But it wasn't fair to Jo Jo. He must not be forgotten.

Jo Jo was a Christmas present I received on my third Christmas. That I don't remember at all. Ironically, he died on the same day three years later.

How horrible it had been for me. How horrible for my parents.

They told me I had spent three years in therapy with a child psychologist.

That I had forgotten too.

CHAPTER 18

Christmas day arrived. We were getting ready to go to Toby's festive going-away party. My parents were invited as well.

Yesterday, when my dad brought the urn to me, he had also brought me a photo album full of pictures of me with Jo Jo. I had never seen this album. They must have hidden it well. Jo Jo did look almost identical to Rosie. No wonder the sight of her had caused such a welling of emotion. The black and tan Cavalier was the rarest color among the breed, and until Rosie, I had never seen another one other than Jo Jo.

As I brushed my hair in front of the vanity I glanced at the windowsill where the potted daisies still bloomed in my childhood bedroom. Jo Jo's little urn sat between two of the pots. There he could look out onto the large backyard where he once played. True, it was no longer the same backyard. It had been extensively renovated over the years. But still, I liked to think that he would enjoy this view.

Oddly, a burden had lifted; a burden I hadn't even realized was there—until I saw that poster of Rosie in the veterinary hospital. My parents had wished to protect me from the horror of that memory. They had always intended to tell me one day, which was why they had kept the urn. But as time passed my mom decided it was best to let the past sleep, which was why she had buried the urn. She had no idea that one day that memory would rise to haunt me.

I don't know if it would have been better had I known sooner what they were hiding. It seemed to have affected the way I formed attachments. I had a very close attachment to my parents, and a very loose one when it came to the men in my life. Until I met Charlie. It astounded me how loving a dog could leave that kind of lasting effect—even when you stopped remembering. It was still buried there, somewhere.

All I know is that it was nobody's fault. Jo Jo was gone.

The clouds drifted in the blue sky. The sun was shining. I liked to think that there really was a 'Rainbow Bridge' where deceased pets crossed to a happy place.

Meanwhile, I had a second chance to make another dog happy.

Lily came bouncing into my room. She was going to meet her new sister today. I squatted and tried to put a Santa hat on her head. She shook it off vigorously. *No thanks, Mama.* I laughed. The little dickens thought clothes were only for people. I would save the hat for Rosie.

Charlie and I took separate cars from my folks. When we arrived, the front door of Toby's gorgeous Ancaster home was open and visitors were freely entering the festively decorated house. A large, white, artificial tree stood in front of an enormous bay window hung with blue, pink, and lavender ornaments.

We went inside and Lily, a little disturbed by the crowd clung close to me.

"Maybe this was a bad idea to bring her to the party," I said to Charlie.

Charlie crouched down to lift Lily up into his arms. "Do you want to go home, little girl?" he asked. She wriggled in his grasp, which meant: *No. Please, put me down.*

The house was full with guests. Toby and Aliisa were popular doctors. They had a lot of friends, all of who had turned out to wish them well in their new life.

Our host himself came towards us, grinning his famous grin. "So glad you could make it, Sophie. Charlie. I was just talking to your parents, Soph. Nice to see them after so long." He shook my fiancé's hand. "Nice to see you again too, Charlie. So glad you could make it. Come, Rosie is in her room. It's too crowded downstairs and we didn't want her to get underfoot and stepped on so we left her upstairs. I'm sure Lily appreciates what I mean." He gave her a pat.

Rosie is in her room?

Toby grinned at my astonished expression. "What? Didn't you know? Rosie has her own bedroom."

I laughed. I hoped this was not going to be a difficult habit to break because in our house she was going to have to share the bedroom with the three of us.

He led us upstairs and Lily frolicked up the dark, gorgeous hardwood stairs, glad to get away from all of the stampeding feet. The top floor was just as immaculately designed as the main floor. Everything seemed new and pristine. The hallway was a pale taupe color with clean white trim as though newly painted. It was lined with modern paintings and pieces of multimedia art like an art gallery. We passed several bedrooms, each showing crisp stylish bedcoverings and contemporary furniture, until we reached one with a shut door. Toby opened it and Rosie leaped off a double bed, covered with a patchwork duvet in pink, white and mint green. It was filled with every imaginable stuffed and rubber doggy toy.

Her favorite babble ball went rolling across the floor. Lily ran to investigate it but Rosie objected and lunged at the ball.

"Rosie," Toby called. "Come meet your new

mommy and daddy."

It was as though she understood. She abandoned the ball, which made a few giggling sounds, attracting Lily's curiosity. Rosie came to me as I extended my arms and placed her chin in my hand. I ruffled the top of her head and kissed her on her silky snout.

I looked up at Charlie and he smiled. She went to him when he called her but Lily wasn't having any of that. As though she plotted it and knew how her new sister felt about the ball she leaped forward and knocked the ball across the room. Well, Rosie could not resist. She shot out of Charlie's grasp and tackled the ball. As she knocked it sideways with her nose, it screeched: "Hot diggity dog!"

"Thanks, Toby," I said, spreading my arms to include the two dogs. "I think this is the best Christmas gift of all."

Toby shook his head. I had called after my meltdown to explain the whole thing, why I had rushed off that day at the gardening center in such distress. He had been very understanding. "No. Thank *you*. I couldn't have asked for a better Christmas present for Rosie."

Noises sounded on the staircase and voices mumbled. Two heads popped in through the doorway, making me stop dead still. Were my eyes deceiving me? Was it some kind of a joke? I threw a glance at Toby but his eyes were turned to the newcomers.

Leo? Leo was here? And—and Abe? What was Abe doing here?

I yanked my attention back to Toby. "You guys all know each other?"

Toby grinned. "Leo is Rosie's regular vet."

My mouth opened slightly. I suppose that should not surprise me. Dundas and Ancaster were joint towns. But Abe?

Toby raised his hands jauntily. "Did you see the kitchen… and the master bathroom?" No, I had not. We had come upstairs first thing after our arrival. "Well, you should go and have a look. All of it is Abe and Kate's handiwork. The job was done—uh—maybe two years ago?" It suddenly dawned on me. That was how Abe and Kate had met. My jaw dropped further. Well, why not?

My focus swung back to the new arrivals. "And Leo and Abe, you know each other because…?" Abe had no dog, so Leo wasn't his veterinarian. *Ah, okay. Got it now.* Leo had just finished having his clinic updated. That was how he knew Abe. Abe was his contractor. Small world.

My eyes lowered to Rosie who had given up the ball and trundled over to me on making eye contact. Her bright gaze brightened even further, her tail slashed to and fro. It was as though she knew that a big change was about to take place in her life and she was okay with it. She was mine if I wanted her. And oh, how I wanted her. I wanted to be her new mama. And I couldn't have made this decision without Charlie's understanding, patience and empathy. The way forward was clear to me now. Leo, Toby and Abe. They were all smiling as I greeted my new dog. They were each really important men in my growth, during a certain period in my life. They were what I had needed then.

And now?

Now, they were the past, just like Jo Jo.

Charlie moved next to Rosie and got down on one knee. He had not proposed this way the first time around because it was too cold and snowy that night at the botanical garden. Today was kind of ideal and we were inside, warm and dry. He brought out the ring. The jeweler had assured him that it was perfect: no flaws, no hairline fracture.

"Sophie—" he began.

I dropped to my knees in front of him, didn't even wait for him to continue. For the first time in a long time I was going to be impulsive. "Yes!" I said.

The dogs rushed in to see what all the excitement was about.

"*Every* time," I promised, eyes shining with tears, "it will be yes."

He slipped the diamond ring on my finger.

I looked up at the three former men in my life. I could have married any one of them. But fate has a strange way of making you sure of your choices and equally sure of your mistakes. Some people bring out the best in you; some people bring out the worst. Charlie brought out the best in me.

Lily squeezed in between us, and then Rosie squeezed in between her.

I laughed. "Merry Christmas, girls."

SPECIAL PREVIEW: FROM **DAPHNE LYNN STEWART'S** NEXT BOOK IN THE CHARMING **MERRY AND BRIGHT SERIES** OF **ROMANTIC CHRISTMAS STORIES FOR PET LOVERS**

The Christmas Castle

CHAPTER ONE

My cat Shakespeare came to me the day my mother died. He was a pure white tomcat, a big boy weighing in at twenty pounds.

He was sitting on my doorstep when I returned home from the funeral. His pose was regal, head held high, ears perked, green eyes sending a piercing gaze demanding of attention. Something about those eyes had me mesmerized. They reminded me of someone, and it only took a few seconds to realize who that was. A combination of warmth and mistrust flooded my senses all at once and I would have burst into tears, except that there was something distressingly comforting about his presence.

Is it true that white cats bring good luck? I was in no condition to debate the truth of that statement.

I shooed him away with my handbag, but he did

not run, as most cats would have, but merely sat there contemplating me. He had no collar or tags, or other identifying items on his person (can a cat be considered a person?) He may have been microchipped, I had no way to tell, and was certain he belonged to someone, although I had never seen him before in my life. I was in no mood to muddle over it. I tried shooing him away again, this time with my foot, but he remained obstinate.

When I unlocked the front door and went inside, he followed me, slipping in around my legs before I could stop him. It was as though he had some purpose. And while I was distraught at Mom's death, it was considerate of the tenacious tom to distract me.

That was four years ago, Christmas Eve. I am thirty-three now and still single. So much for white cats bringing good luck. I don't know if my relationship status has anything to do with Shakespeare. He doesn't think anyone is good enough for me. He turns up his tail at anyone who comes to the door and is even ruder to anyone who tries to enter the house. He still waits for me every afternoon when I arrive home from work. Not outside of course. He has become an indoor cat, a *neutered* indoor cat—after I learned he was a stray—but I see him in the window as I hurry up the walk, and I *must* hurry because after all it is his dinnertime, and if you own a cat, you know what I mean. The cat runs the household. And a cat has got to eat!

I am a teacher of historical literature. My favorite author is Alexandre Dumas and my favorite book is *The Three Musketeers*. But I named the cat Shakespeare because of his seeming command of the world and his catty sense of humor. I don't mean that he was spiteful (can an animal be spiteful?). No, I mean that if he were a human boy, he would have had a clever tongue like Puck in *A Midsummer Night's Dream*. Hmm, maybe I should have named him Puck? But no, Shakespeare suits him so much better. He is the ringmaster of the show, the conductor of the symphony, the director of the play. It is with him my world revolves, as we write our historical novel. After all he was there when I got my job in the English department at Dalhousie University here in the beautiful seaside city of Halifax. I wish Mom could have been there. She would have been so proud. But as I observe Shakespeare and receive his knowing look in return, I believe that perhaps she was.

So, I have no time for dating or serious relationships. When not teaching, I am writing a romantic adventure novel. Like the kind of thing Dumas wrote only set in a Gothic castle.

I have never been inside a Gothic castle. So, it is ironic that when I returned home today, and checked my mailbox, I discovered I had inherited one.

Let me be clear. It isn't exactly a medieval castle. The Gothic castle I allegedly inherited is actually a grand mansion designed by Scottish architect James Balfour and built in 1881. It belongs—or should I say *belonged*—to my grandfather, a man I never met because he had a falling out with his only child, my mom, before I was born.

What the disagreement was about I never knew. When I was old enough to ask my mother refused to talk about it, and when I questioned Dad, he was just as stubborn. So, by the time I reached my teen years I stopped asking.

Dad passed away in a diving accident a few years before my mom, whom I believe died from a broken heart—although the doctors say it was a congenital heart defect. My only surviving relative was my grandfather. And now it seems I will never meet him. He died three days ago, leaving the estate to me. The letter the lawyer sent to me was succinct:

Julie Bramblea
33 Sea Court Road
Halifax, Nova Scotia

September 24, 20XX

Dear Ms. Bramblea,

I am writing with regard to your late grandfather Blaine Alan Mackenzie's last wishes. Sadly, he passed away in his home September 21. He has bequeathed his ancestral home Ravenscliffe Castle to you his only grandchild, Julie Mackenzie Bramblea, daughter of Jenna Paisley Mackenzie and William Garth Bramblea under two conditions: 1) that you take possession of the estate before December 24, Christmas Eve of this year. And 2) that you keep and care for his cat, named Xian, until her natural death.

The stipulations of this inheritance are that you make Ravenscliffe your permanent and primary residence, and that you provide for the cat. The cat is not to be rehomed or otherwise removed from the property except for veterinary visits if required, or emergency situations that might threaten her life if she remains on the premises.

If you are unable or unwilling to fulfill either of the conditions (outlined in greater detail in the will), the estate will be bequeathed to the city of Hamilton (where the property is located) in the province of Ontario to serve as the future home of the Hamilton History Museum, and you will be removed as legatee. All liquid assets will be transferred to the city for its renovation and upkeep.

Should you require further clarification or assistance in making your decision, please do not hesitate to contact me. My firm has handled your grandfather's legal matters for forty years. I look forward to hearing from you. And, I might add, the sooner I hear from you the better.

My firm sends its deepest condolences for your loss.

Best regards,

Alec Forester
Law Firm of Forester, Long & Jameson

The letter read like an ultimatum. My eyes were wide as saucers as I stared at the unbelievable missive pinched between my cold fingers. Shakespeare leaped onto the bare, wooden dining room table where I had been sifting through my mail, and sat coolly observing my reaction to the lawyer's letter.

My reaction could be described most simply as stunned. Why had my grandfather not reached out to me earlier? Preferably while he was still alive?

I had forgotten I even had a grandfather. I have no other relatives, no cousins, aunts or uncles that I am aware of. It had never occurred to me to seek him out. I had no address for him. Only a first name and a last name. I suppose I could have Googled him but it never crossed my mind to do so. I had no idea that he was a recluse living in a castle.

I stroked Shakespeare's silky head and he pulled away. I was only allowed to pet him when he requested the attention, and he had not. I smiled at my stately companion.

"Well, Shakespeare, what do you think? Would you like to live in a castle and meet the feline who apparently owns it?"

Shakespeare licked his paws nonchalantly, gave me a glare with his all-seeing eyes. It was almost as though it were my mom's knowing eyes that peered out at me through that haughty feline face.

Every time I had asked her about her father, "No" was all she said.

Shakespeare lifted his tail as he stood up on all fours and swung his backside towards me.

It was clear what *his* answer was.

However, Shakespeare was only a cat, opinionated or not. Ultimately, the choice was mine.

I required practically no time at all to come to my decision. It was as though Dumas was speaking to me himself: *Never fear quarrels, but seek hazardous adventures.* Quote. End quote.

Three months. That was all I had to make my decision and move. Or give it all up.

It didn't take me three months or even three days. I ignored the cat's disapproving gaze. Three minutes was all it took to make up my mind.

"I get it, Shakespeare," I commiserated. "You've placed your vote. Too bad. You know the rules. Where I go, you go."

And like the three musketeers (except that there were only the two of us) I rallied all of my courage and resolve. *All for one, and one for all.*

About the Author

Christmas is my favourite time of year, because that is when I found my "forever guy," and so I will always equate Christmas with love. Most of my stories take place during the festive season, sometimes in small towns and sometimes in the big city, and everything is always Merry and Bright (although it may not start out that way) and love and happiness are possible for anyone.

I am mainly a novelist but have also written heartwarming stories for the popular series Chicken Soup for the Soul under the name of Deborah Cannon.

I currently have two series. So, on your summer holidays, stretch out in your backyard or on the beach, pour yourself a cool glass of wine and indulge in a SUMMER DESTINY romance. As autumn fades to winter cuddle up with your fur baby by a roaring fire on a cold day with a cup of hot cocoa and enjoy one of my cozy MERRY AND BRIGHT holiday love stories.

For anyone who is curious as to who those cute pets are on the covers of my Christmas romances, they are all pets of either my friends or my family. So those cuties are real! Sadly, some have passed away now. My precious Ming and Tang are gone, but I have my new furbabies Luke and Lucy. I dedicate these love stories to my beloved dogs, past and present.

Books by Daphne Lynn Stewart:

All She Wants for Christmas

All NYC publicist Belle Rice and her best friend, bestselling romance author Cate Zarcova, want is to re-experience the white Christmas of their childhood in a quiet countryside estate. When Belle rescues a runaway dog and returns it to its owner Christopher Winters, cupid strikes and Belle falls hard, not only for Chris but also for the little dog. Only one thing impedes her happiness. Chris is a recent widow, with a new girlfriend. He owns a once lucrative Christmas tree farm now fallen to corporate competition, which is threatening him with bankruptcy. His one dream is to keep alive his dead wife's shelter for abandoned pets, but without the income from the tree farm the shelter will have to close. Is there a place for Belle in this tangled relationship?

http://www.amazon.com/All-She-Wants-Christmas-lovers-ebook/dp/B00QMTZURQ/

Christmas in June

Leigh and Matthew were best friends from childhood who met at her grandmother's lakeside cottage in a charming tourist town every Christmas. They dated throughout high school and now, fifteen years later Leigh is a renowned reporter and Matt owns the Little Inn at Bayfield. They have not seen each other since graduating from high school. Leigh is in town to visit her grandmother, and finds in the attic a time capsule that she and Matt put together when they were fourteen years old. When she meets him again, she learns that he is engaged and that his inn is in trouble. Leigh's plan is to advertise Christmas in Bayfield via a documentary. Although it is June, sunny and warm, she is determined to dress up the town in holiday style to film. Matt, she decides will be the star of her show, and against her will she finds her attraction to him rekindled.

http://www.amazon.com/Christmas-June-lovers-Bright-Romance-ebook/dp/B010MQQYJC

The Christmas Mix-up
On the eve of the Christmas season Danica Meriweather picks up the wrong pet carrier at her local airport, and is thrust face to face with the man of her dreams. Only thing is: she never really saw his face. He was gone with *her* pet carrier before she knew what had happened and all she remembers of him is his tall, handsome form disappearing into a limousine with her dog. Now she has *his* dog. Sam Forrest is a wonderful man with an eight-year-old daughter whom Danica falls in love with. And although she has met his daughter, she has yet to meet him in the flesh. But love blossoms between them nonetheless. Meanwhile Danica's catering business, which is run from her home—a heritage

building—is threatened by a ruthless corporation. Her only hope is to convince the company's CEO the value of historic homes. She agrees to cater his corporate Christmas party despite mixed feelings, and soon learns why her feelings are mixed.

http://www.amazon.com/Christmas-Mix-Up-lovers-Bright-Romance-ebook/dp/B0116H9IF8

The Christmas Bunny
Kendra Tyler has big dreams, one of which includes becoming a professor of animal behavior. In order to accomplish her dream, she needs to go to grad school, and in order to pay for school she needs a good part-time job. This she finds at the Bunny Club in Toronto. Her other dream is to marry the wonderful man she's dating. Cabe Alexander is rich and powerful and has her destiny in his hands. But another powerful man, Nicholas Marley is waiting on the sidelines to shake up her destiny, someone whom she least expected to throw a wrench into her plans.

http://www.amazon.com/Christmas-Bunny-lovers-Bright-Romance-ebook/dp/B016E7VRG8

Dashing Through the Snow
When Chelsea Doll meets Jason Frost she realizes she is engaged to the wrong brother. She and Bryce are planning their Christmas Eve wedding

at Langdon Hall a luxury country estate hotel. Bryce is a stockbroker in Toronto and Chelsea is an executive risk analyst whose secret dream is to run her own florist shop. Jason is a local business owner who runs *Dashing Through The Snow (or sun)*, a horse and carriage business for weddings, and corporate and community events. It seems she and Bryce's brother have everything in common including a love of dogs. If only she had met him first.

https://www.amazon.com/Dashing-Through-Snow-lovers-Romance-ebook/dp/B01I1V7JQ2?ie=UTF8&*Version*=1&*entries*=0#nav-subnav

A Very Catty Christmas
Budding artist Lorelei Channing is in love with art curator Harry Snow. But he doesn't know she exists. By day she is Lori Channing, a docent at the Art Gallery of Hamilton; by night she is textile artiste *Lorelei*. Due to a mix up, Lorelei has won a contest to have one of her pieces exhibited in a prestigious art show, whose opening night is Christmas Eve. The director of her gallery dislikes her because her cat keeps escaping from their loft near the gallery, to wreak havoc with the museum shop's Christmas decorations. When Harry finally notices her because of her artwork, he still doesn't know that she is the bumbling docent his mother complains of. Between Lori's mistakes and Giselle's

mischief Madam director begins to have suspicions and Lorelei begins to wonder whether she's dating the right man.

https://www.amazon.com/Very-Catty-Christmas-lovers-Romance-ebook/dp/B01IAKI6IY?ie=UTF8&*Version*=1&*entries*=0

Rocky Mountain Christmas
What would you do if you fell in love with your cousin's boyfriend? Joy Zamboni is a magazine writer. Her Christmas assignment? To produce an article about how dogs are replacing men in the loves of modern women. To aid in her research she has adopted a rescue dog. The dog is skittish and does not trust her, and runs halfway down the block before stopping. They play this game for ten minutes until a charming fellow appears out of nowhere and shows Joy how to win the dog's confidence. His name is Jack and he owns a canine training school. Joy is so smitten that she enrolls the dog in classes, and has the guts to ask Jack if she can interview him for her article. Are his feelings mutual? They plan to meet again after the holidays but when Joy arrives at her family's mountain resort in the Rockies her dear cousin Ellie is there with her boyfriend—Jack.

https://www.amazon.com/Rocky-Mountain-Christmas-lovers-Romance-ebook/dp/B01ICBESP6?ie=UTF8&*Version*=1&*entries*=0

Christmastime in the City
Romance bookstore owner, Olivia Snow, has a serious choice to make. When the godlike sous-chef at the French bistro next door saves her cat Nilly from the top of a lamppost in the quaint town of Dundas, Olivia believes her months-old feud with him is over. She believes that maybe she has feelings for him until her younger sister Gabrielle beats her to the punch. They both need dates for their cousin Darla's Christmas wedding at a chateau near Paris. Winter in Paris and a castle wedding is a dream-come-true. When sister Gabby steals her date, Olivia is desperate to find another and settles for Hank a wine connoisseur and manager of her local liquor store. Yeah, pretty ordinary guy, she thinks, but boy is she ever wrong!

https://www.amazon.com/Christmastime-City-lovers-Bright-Romance-ebook/dp/B07GZ44PY9/ref=sr_1_3?s=digital-text&ie=UTF8&qid=1538593605&sr=1-3

Mistletoe Inn
Laurel Westlake is furious when Tom Holiday the owner of a Niagara winery almost runs over her dogs Bella and Daisy in a hotel parking lot in the tourist town of Niagara-on-the-lake. She has just learned that the hotel can't take her because of a burst water main. Now she's late for a meeting

with a very important client for her aunt's party planning business. She is supposed to plan an opulent Christmas party for the town's big-time realtor. Worse, as she's leaving the parking lot, she crashes her car into a crate of expensive wine that Tom is unloading. How is she going to pay for it? She's frustrated, he's mad, but when she injures herself on a piece of bottle glass Tom shows true compassion. He tells her she can pay him when she can and invites her back to his winery to recuperate from her horrible day. She is falling for him, but then she learns that he's already dating someone. Someone from her past…

https://www.amazon.com/Mistletoe-Inn-Lovers-Bright-Romance-ebook/dp/B07GZ7YXMJ/ref=sr_1_2?s=digital-text&ie=UTF8&qid=1538595420&sr=1-2

Let it Snow
It's love at first sight on a snowy winter's day in early December when Joe Douglas and Noelle Hollyburn meet at her cousin's veterinary practice in Ottawa Ontario. Noelle is a pet photographer. Joe's dog has peed on her and she has to change out of her soiled clothing and wear her cousin Nicola's lab coat. It just happens to have the name Dr. Nicola Hollyburn, DVM stitched on it. When Wealthy advertising executive Joe Douglas arrives to pick up his bulldog, he mistakes Noelle for Nicola, the vet.

Joe asks her on a date. At Noelle's pleading, Nicola agrees to allow Noelle to pretend to be her. It is too late for Noelle to correct him now that they are dating, but her luck can only last so long before he finds out who she really is.

https://www.amazon.com/Let-Snow-Lovers-Bright-Romance-ebook/dp/B07GZM16SZ/ref=sr_1_1?s=digital-text&ie=UTF8&qid=1538595420&sr=1-1

It Wouldn't be Christmas Without You
When Abby Hollybrook's high school crush Max Granger returns at Christmas with two dogs he needs to rehome, Abby knows that the troublesome pups are about to change her life. Her landlady hates the dogs and she hates Abby. Fortunately, she doesn't hate Max. Max's rented house no longer allows dogs and Abby's landlady jumps at the chance to find him a new place—preferably by her side. Abby must keep her rescue center open and train Max's dogs. But will it be enough? Will Abby and Max get together by Christmas or will Abby's landlady force them apart?

https://www.amazon.com/Wouldnt-Christmas-Without-You-Romance-ebook/dp/B08PN6QGZK/ref=sr_1_5?dchild=1&qid=1620419777&refinements=p_27%3ADaphne+Lynn+Stewart&s=digital-text&sr=1-5&text=Daphne+Lynn+Stewart

Three Nights Before Christmas

After accidentally pepper spraying herself *and* her fiancé's dog in a cooking accident, Sophie Star has a nightmare that her engagement ring cracks in half. The next morning couldn't get any worse. When she takes the dog to the vet, she discovers that he is her high school boyfriend. And when she goes to see the eye doctor, he happens to be ex number two. To top it off, ex number three turns out to be her parents' contractor! Are these blasts from the past warning her not to marry Charlie? Or do they have something to do with a dog she can't remember but loved as a child?

https://www.amazon.com/Three-Nights-Before-Christmas-Romance-ebook/dp/B094DXZ6DB/ref=sr_1_1?dchild=1&qid=1620672201&refinements=p_27%3ADaphne+Lynn+Stewart&s=digital-text&sr=1-1&text=Daphne+Lynn+Stewart

The Christmas Castle

Julie Bramblea's estranged grandfather died leaving her a Gothic castle and a mystery to solve. Why did her mother run away to marry Julie's father and never reconnect with her family again? When her cat Shakespeare goes missing all of the pieces start to fall into place as she falls for her newly retained lawyer and his little boy.

https://www.amazon.com/Christmas-Castle-lovers-Bright-Romance-ebook/dp/B094NW94ST/ref=sr_1_1?dchild=1&keywords=The+Christmas+Castle+Daphne+Lynn+Stewart&qid=1631651476&s=digital-text&sr=1-1

Christmas in September
When April Snow meets Sam Fir and his teenaged daughter, she learns that love is synonymous with 'home.' Lifestyle journalist April is assigned to pen an article plugging Sam's new mashup business, a coffeehouse/art gallery/bookshop. Instead, she finds herself in a game of deception where she helps Sam's daughter hide the fact that she is keeping a dog in their condo without his knowledge. Will this destroy April's chances at romance with Sam or can she help make a young girl happy without jeopardizing her relationship with the father?

https://www.amazon.com/gp/product/B0BMWBYDTX?ref_=dbs_m_mng_rwt_calw_tkin_13&storeType=ebooks

Tang's Christmas Miracle
Marilee Christian's world is falling apart. She has no love life. Her junior assistant is scheming to steal her job. And her precious little dog has been

diagnosed with cancer. Only a life-saving operation can keep him alive and give him a chance for a future. This surgery is only available at the OVC, a special animal hospital in Guelph Ontario, where their specialists are in high demand. Because of her deep love for this dog, because of all the joy he brings to people and animals alike, Marilee promises to sacrifice her ambitions—if it will allow Tang to live. When all seems lost, a chance meeting with Joel, a man Tang mistook for Marilee's brother, helps her decide. Joel is kind and good, a veterinarian from Toronto. Tang is kind and good, an innocent dog whose destiny opens Marilee's heart to the truth about love—a truth that her dog always knew.

https://www.amazon.com/gp/product/B0CLFFH11S?ref_=dbs_m_mng_rwt_calw_tkin_14&storeType=ebooks&qid=1720558986&sr=1-9

A Puck Bunny Christmas
Former puck bunny Angel Turtledove reunites with high school classmate, ex-hockey star Barry Shepard at her daughter's birthday party. Her daughter's pet bunny is missing and the party is outdoors in a park in the middle of winter. Angel realizes what it is like for the homeless, especially around Christmas. She has seen it first hand with a woman she befriended, who lives in a tent at

the park. When she learns that Barry has not only rescued her daughter's lost bunny, but that his dream is to build homes for the homeless, she is smitten. As she struggles to convince her wealthy ex-husband and girlfriend to finance Barry's project, she finds that the girlfriend is not only blocking her blossoming romance with Barry, but that she is dead set on getting rid of the homeless neighbor. That neighbor has a secret. And it has something to do with her.

NEW SERIES:
Summer Destiny Romance

Paradise on Deck: A Summer Destiny Romance
Do you believe in destiny? Ariel Stone does not until she meets handsome deck and landscape designer Ben Hammer on a cruise ship. Ariel is aboard the *Crystal Serenity* redecorating one of their exclusive penthouse suites (Yes, this ocean liner has penthouses!) when she experiences a decorating emergency. Ben comes to the rescue leaving Ariel wondering how it is that he knows exactly what to do and has the equipment to do it. He refuses payment for the job so she invites him to join her for a drink. While together they make a promise not to tell each other anything about their personal lives, but instead to play a 'game' that Ben calls Destiny. "If it's meant to be we will meet again," he promises.

https://www.amazon.com/Paradise-Deck-Summer-Destiny-Romance-ebook/dp/B01IE0IVB2/ref=sr_1_3?s=digital-text&ie=UTF8&qid=1473184274&sr=1-3#nav-subnav

If Not For You: A Summer Destiny Romance
When a man loves a woman, he will go to any extent to win her, but to what extent will he go to save her life? Leanne Constance meets Andy Briggs at a psychology conference in L.A. They both study relationships and the subject of "Love". They hit it off and spend one night together in a luxurious room at the Beverly Hills hotel, where her most precious moment is waking up on a sunny, breezy morning and having breakfast with him on their private patio overflowing with bougainvillea. Only one thing stands in the way of happily ever after. He lives in Berkeley California and she lives in Toronto, Canada. Leanne has a secret, a serious health condition. Can Andy live with this? After months of a long-distance relationship, Andy asks Leanne to marry him. When Andy discovers Leanne's secret, he is horrified that he might lose her. Can he save her, and if he does, at what cost?

https://www.amazon.com/If-Not-You-Destiny-Romance-ebook/dp/B01M1EDZ2R/ref=sr_1_1?s=digital-text&ie=UTF8&qid=1473857825&sr=1-1#nav-

subnav

Manufactured by Amazon.ca
Bolton, ON